Drinking With God

Derek Pittman

from various sources. Please consult a licensed professional before attempting any techniques outlined in this book.

By reading this document, the reader agrees that under no circumstances is the author responsible for any losses, direct or indirect, that are incurred as a result of the use of the information contained within this document, including, but not limited to, errors, omissions, or inaccuracies.

Table of Contents

Introduction

A lot of times, we look at God like this all-powerful figure, or some kid with an ant farm watching us for amusement. Playing with us and our emotions. What if the church is right, and we're created in his image and likeness, all flaws and imperfections included? As you read the Bible, if you look at it from the view of God as a father trying to raise his children, it creates a unique perspective. What if God is more human like than we think, and the Bible is the story of an entity who is trying to raise his kids? He loses his temper, he tries to explain stuff that goes way over our heads, but it's all with a purpose, and he does it because he cares. This is not a statement from the Catholic church or a doctoral thesis on God, just a different perspective portrayed in a fictional novel meant to bring a new perspective to the Man on High.

Chapter 1:

Waking Up

He parks his car after a long day of work. He sighs and smiles that he's finally home. When he looks up, he sees his wife standing there on the porch, her hands on her mouth. He studies her in the dim evening light and sees that she's distressed, about to cry.

"Babe? What's wrong?"

"Oh, honey…" She whimpers and runs to pull him into her arms.

After holding her for a while, she pulls away and waves him inside. Upon entering his house, he sees his brother, his mother, his children, and his niece and nephew.

"What's going on, guys?" He smiles awkwardly. "Someone do something illegal? Was it me?"

His brother walks up and hugs him. "Dad just had a massive heart attack. He didn't even make it to the hospital."

He gapes at his brother, hugging him and everyone else in the room.

"Dad?" is all he can manage before he opens his eyes.

The sun beams into Gabriel Johnson's eyes as he lies in bed, opening them from the dream he's re-lived for years now. He turns over and tries to go back to sleep, but he can't. He decides to get up and get ready for work. He stumbles from the bed, and his head is spinning. He looks around and sees his wife is gone, left for work an hour ago. The kids are not making any noise, and he assumes they are at school now. He waits a few minutes for his head to stop spinning and then he gets himself dressed.

"Time for some breakfast." Gabe goes into the kitchen and pulls out a bottle of whiskey. He pours himself some coffee and then puts a shot of whiskey into it. Breakfast of champions. He pulls out a slice of bread from the bread box and toasts it. Once it pops, he takes it with him to his car, as well as a small mickey of vodka. He drives to work early and sits in his car in the parking lot. Gabe stared at the mickey in his hand. Part of him is against the decision he is about to make, and then he looks up at the sign for his workplace.

He drinks back the vodka like it's water, finishing it on the spot, gets out of the car, and stumbles into the mechanic garage. He sways as he walks, but he tries to hide it from the few morning workers he sees. He always tries to get there early, so he can get in a nap. He almost falls into his station and tries sitting on the chair, finding it uncomfortable. He lays himself on the floor and dozes off before he realizes it.

"Ain't this a sight for sore eyes! Asleep before lunch, this must be a record," Gabe hears the voice through the drunken haze his mind is clouded in. He opens his eyes and sees the blurred image of his boss, Phil, standing over him with his arms crossed. After a few seconds, his eyes focus a little more, and he can see the man more clearly. He is lying under the desk of his station. Phil squats down and shakes him awake, assuming he's still asleep. "Come to my office. Now, Gabe."

Phil stands up and slams the door; the sound crashes into Gabriel's consciousness, no different than Phil's voice a few seconds earlier. He looks around, taking in his surroundings, then crawls slowly from under the desk, hitting his head on the way through. All he wanted was a nap, but he realizes he's probably been doing that a little too frequently. He groans in pain and crumples.

"I'm getting too old for this…" Gabriel says as he uses the chair to clumsily help himself up. He stumbles his way from the office and towards Phil's office. He knocks on the door, and Phil hollers for him to come in. Gabriel opens the door and does his best not to stumble, but it's harder than he thought. His head is spinning. He catches himself on the chair and sits down. Phil sighs heavily and massages his temples.

"Gabe, I took you on here because you know the job, and your brother was a big influence. He sold me on you, and you did deliver, in the beginning." Phil seems to be trying to keep his voice from shouting at Gabe as he explains his thoughts. "But you have disappointed me again and again, coming to work drunk for months on end; we're lucky to get you sober on any day, and frankly, this isn't going to fly anymore. You're done; take your things and get out."

Gabriel slurs, "At least I'm coming to work…"

"You know that's not the point, and I'm not listening to excuses!" Phil shouts. "You're fired!"

Gabriel sighs heavily, gets up slowly, and leaves the office. He stumbles back to his small desk and slumps into the chair. He drinks heavily from his water bottle in an attempt to sober up, and it helps a little as he gathers up all of his things. He shakes the thoughts from his head and puts all of his things into a box; only a few pens and pencils, his favorite wrench, and the pictures of his family. As he packs up the pictures, he finds himself stopping to look at them. The first is a photo of himself and his wife, Anna, on their wedding day. He sighs and remembers clearly how beautiful she looked. The next is a family photo of them with their three children, 12-year-old Kayla, 10-year-old Jefferey, and 7-year-old Meaghan at a park making funny faces. Another is of him and Kayla when she was a baby, crawling all over him like a little monkey. He finishes packing up and carefully carries the box to his car. On the way, the other employees watch him go, shaking their heads shamefully as they work.

"Good riddance, slacker!" one guy yells.

However, there were a few who were less harsh. At least some of them cared.

"Hope you can clean yourself up, man." Gabriel looks up and sees Steve, one of the customer service workers, waving at him.

"Well, at least there's someone who likes me here…" Gabriel grumbles. He makes it to his car and places the box in his trunk, sitting in the driver's seat and starting the car. He takes one last look at the mechanic business. The big garages, the vehicles on the lifts being worked on. He sighs and drives off after sobering up.

His destination is his favorite bar, The Thirsty Traveler. The place has the vibe of an Irish pub and a billiards bar all squished into one. The bar is situated between a pharmacy and a pet store. There is a sign on the façade with the subtitle, *"Bar none the best ale in town."* Another is jutting out and hanging from a small iron bar. He parks his car, locks it, and enters. The smell of beer and fried food embraces his nostrils, and he feels at ease. This bar is his second home.

"Honey, I'm home," he mutters to himself. "Not a bad crowd for Wednesday night."

He can almost hear the first few bars of Billy Joel's "Piano Man" as he walks through the bar.

The tables are filled with customers and families chatting and enjoying their evening meal. Gabe walks up to the bar and takes a seat. The bartender nods at him as he walks by with a drink and a tray of food. The best part of this bar is that it's 2 miles from Gabe's house, so he never has to drive far to get home, if he even remembers where his car is. He could even walk if he wanted to. He'd done that many times after forgetting he left his car there. He cringes, remembering how Anna has chewed him out about that before.

"Be right with ya, Gabe!" the bartender says.

"No problem, Doug, take your time." Gabe shifts in his stool. Doug serves the customer he was walking towards and stops in front of Gabe. Doug is a big, burly, bald man who manages the bar.

"The usual?" Doug asks.

"Straight up." Gabe gestures upward with a thumb's up.

"Heavy-duty today...get fired again?" Doug raises an eyebrow. "Show up drunk...again?"

"Who's paying the tab here?" Gabe raises his eyebrow. The two men stare at each other for a moment before pointing at each other and laughing.

"I'm just sayin', something you might want to work on." Doug shrugs. "I've known you a long time, and I'm never going to say no to your company, but you might need to get something figured out."

"I'm good," Gabe assures him.

"As long as you don't blame *me* for being drunk, I'm washing my hands of this. You just be good tonight. I don't want any funny business." Doug keeps his finger up, pointing at Gabe in a warning gesture. He goes off to the cabinet and grabs a bottle of Jack Daniels, setting it in front of Gabe with a shot glass.

"Me? Funny business?" Gabe gestures to himself. Doug uses two fingers to gesture to his eyes then back to Gabe as if to say, *I'm watching you…*

Gabe rolls his eyes and opens the bottle of whiskey to pour himself a shot. He drinks it down in one gulp, feeling the sweet burn of the alcohol along with the flavor. He pulls out his phone to call his brother Andre, but the phone is already ringing in his hands. Andre's number and caller ID flash onto the screen and Gabriel groans, taking another sip before answering.

"Hello?"

"Where are you?" Andre's voice came through the receiver. "Why is it so noisy? Lots of cars to fix today?"

"Did you call to ask something significant or to ask about my day?" Gabe takes another sip.

"You're not at work, are you?" Andre's voice lost all casual tone.

"I am…" Gabe looks around him, continuing to play it off.

"Does a mechanic shop have clinking glasses and conversation?" Andre is deadly serious.

"It's, uh, I'm drinking with the boys…during the day," Gabe answers. "Had a successful day, and the boss took us out and sliced early."

"You were fired, weren't you?" Andre's tone of voice is louder than before.

Gabe sighs. "I just said we're out for drinks…"

"Gabe, you are the worst liar. I'm coming to get you." Andre hangs up before Gabe can respond. Gabe looks at his phone and nods in defeat. He downs a nice long sip of his drink and prepares for the hell he's about to face from Andre. Doug approaches Gabe.

"Everything okay, man?" He dries a glass while he speaks. "That looked like a heavy phone call."

"That was my brother...I really screwed up this time." Gabe drinks again and holds his face in his hands. "If Anna finds out, I don't know if I can keep her around. I can't lose those kids…"

"I know, man." Doug nods to him. "I know how much you love them."

"I do," Gabe shakes his head. "You know, all the time I've spent here rather than at home with them…"

"Yep, that I know too," Doug chuckles. "You've almost drunk me out of stock with the number of times you've been here. Remember that one time I had to kick you out because you and your brother were asleep here for hours?"

"That was one good nap, though." Gabe sips his drink and points at Doug.

"Well, I guess it helped one of us out." He goes off to serve another customer and then comes back to Gabe.

"How is Andre, by the way?" Doug asks, leaning against the bar as Gabe refills the shot glass and drinks it down.

"He's still the big shot he's always been."

"Isn't he an accountant at that big company?"

"No need to rub it in…"

"Sorry man, didn't mean to," Doug sighs. "I wish I could have that life."

"What, and never serve me drinks again?" Gabe holds his hands out. "What would I do without you?"

"Use another bartender that works here?"

"You're the only one who's nice to me." Gabe nods. He hears a snicker from down the bar.

Gabe looks over and sees a man with a brownish beard with some white in it, and short brown hair. He was wearing a flannel shirt and jeans. The type of guy who worked in trades, casual but comfortable for their line of work. He was just some guy out for drinks after a slow day.

"Oh, I'm sorry, gentlemen. I was just overhearing." He waves his hand and nods. "I meant no offense; carry on." He has a glass of high end whiskey on the rocks, and he sipped from it after speaking, minding his own business. Gabe figures the guy made enough money in his profession that he could afford the good stuff. He is a bit jealous.

"That's all right, it *was* funny." Gabe cocks his head at Doug.

"Not my fault the others don't like you when you come in here." He sighs. "You're not always the most pleasant drunk."

"Depends on my mood; I can be a charmer." Gabe winks and Doug rolls his eyes.

"So, was I right?"

"Right about what?"

"Were you fired? Anna and you had a fight? Andre didn't sound very happy on the phone," Doug asks, legitimately concerned.

"If you must know, yes I was; happy?" Gabe shoots another glass of Jack Daniels. "I got too drunk here last night and I never stopped. Showed up to work early and fell asleep. I guess it was the last straw."

"Can't say I blame them."

Gabe shot him a drunken glare, one eye narrowed. "Nice to know you're in my court."

"You gotta admit it, man, would you appreciate it if a dude takes advantage of precious company time and comes in drunk and unable to work, multiple times, and it's a problem?" Doug asks. "Would you like that?"

"I know I wouldn't." The voice of the odd stranger. Gabe glares over at him.

"Do you mind, sir, we're having a private conversation," Gabe snaps.

"Not very private if it's in a public place." The man shrugs, a glint of mischief in his eye.

"You're not very aware of social rules, are you?" Gabe glares at him and leans over towards him. "What's your deal?"

"Hey, Gabe, simmer down." Doug pats his arm. Gabe shrugs him off.

"I don't like how this dick is eavesdropping on our conversation. This is private stuff!" Gabe hits his shot glass down, making a noise, but not enough to break it, to Doug's relief.

"Gabe, cool it," Doug whispers. "I don't wanna have to kick you out to be at the mercy of your wife in all this mess."

"No, tell me why you're spying on me…" Gabe yells, shrugging off Doug yet again.

"I'm not spying on you, kid." The man smiles and shrugs. "I'm just sitting here and you're talking."

"Well…stop listening!" Gabe drinks back another shot and sticks his tongue out at the man. The look of relief on Doug's face is palpable.

"That was terrifying," he says.

"What was? I find it terrifying that this man was hearing everything about my life."

Doug sighs. "I gotta get back to work, but I'm watching you, Gabe."

"I'm the best behaved dude here!"

Chapter 2:

Andre's Here

Andre storms into the bar, and Gabe hears his footsteps approach him. Gabe doesn't turn around.

"Godspeed, my man…" Doug mutters, pushing a shot glass towards him and going to serve another customer. Gabe pours another shot and downs it, hissing at the burn and preparing for the lecture he's in for.

"I can't freaking believe you…" Andre sits on the stool beside Gabe. "Gabriel Aaron Johnson…"

"Oh, you know my full name. I guess you really are my brother." Gabe pours a little more into the glass and sips it this time. Gabe puts on his face of nonchalance and apathy. Pretending he doesn't care is easier than facing the truth.

"Cut the crap, you went to work drunk again, didn't you?" Gabe sees Andre turn to face him in the corner of his eye. "How many times do you need to lose a job before you learn?"

"Enough to keep it interesting." Gabe takes a sip again.

"Will you look at me, for God's sake!"

Gabe heaves a deep sigh, finishes the glass of whiskey, and looks at his brother. Andre is a slim man with the physique of someone that does more exercise than just walking. Much more healthy-looking than Gabe's 'fabulous' dad bod.

"Happy?" Gabe raises an eyebrow. "I'm looking at your ugly face, and now I want to drink more." Andre ignores his brother's tone and continues.

"Gabe, you can't keep doing this. I got you that mechanic job thinking you were actually ready to change." Andre's brow furrowed and he ran a hand through his short hair. "This is the third job in a row. If this happens again, I won't be doing this for you anymore."

"Nothing suits me." Gabe shrugs and pours another glass of whiskey for himself.

"How can you be like this?" Andre pulls out his phone and brings up a picture of Gabe and his family as he speaks. "You have a wonderful wife and three of the cutest kids I have ever known, apart from mine, of course…"

Gabe looks at the photo and then quickly pulls his eyes away. "They're fine."

"What will she do if she finds out this happened again?"

"Okay, I get it, I'm a screw-up. I admit it; are you happy now?" Gabe turns to Andre again and finishes his glass.

"Dad dies, and you think you can just go off and act out for this long just because you're sad? He was my father too, and I'm not a freaking child." Andre sighs again. "You used to be so dedicated…to your job, to your family, and Mom after Dad died. What happened to you?"

"Yeah, well, things change." Gabe is drinking from the bottle now, and Doug glances at him and brings his hand to his face. "We can't all be big shot accountants like you, Andre."

"Don't even start…" Andre points a warning finger at Gabe.

"You were always the better looking one, the more successful one; you even got married before I did, and *I'm* the older sibling." Gabe confronts Andre, gesturing his hands in exasperation.

"Gabe, you are a father; you have children and a wife to provide for. Grow up and start acting like it!" Andre gets up to leave, and Gabe grabs his arm.

"Hey, come on, I'm sorry. At least have a drink. You still drink soda, right? It's been a while since we hung out."

"It's been three months. We went out for dinner when you got this job, and now you've blown it. Again. No thanks." Andre pushes Gabe's arm off.

"Just one; sit down." Gabe drinks again and gestures to the chair. "Like old times."

"Old times?" Andre snaps. "Those 'old times' got me in big trouble with my wife and my own issues. I am not about to ride that roller coaster again."

"More for me then." Gabe pours a shot and drinks it. He takes a moment to enjoy the whiskey again, feeling it burn and reveling in it. It almost makes him forget the reason his brother is here.

"There you go again, trying to pretend everything is fine. Well it's not, and you only have yourself to blame." Andre holds his hands out in a defeated gesture. "You're still having that nightmare, aren't you?"

Gabe freezes and closes off immediately. "Who says I am?"

"Your face, that's what," Andre shouts.

"So mature. Aren't you being a little childish here, yelling in a bar?" Gabe turns to him. A few people are staring at them now. Andre doesn't seem to care.

"You need to get help, Gabe, and this denial is only going to make it worse!" Andre pleads. "Get therapy, go to an AA meeting, *something*. It helped me, and it could help you, if you let it. For the sake of your family, Gabe."

Andre sits closer to him and touches his arm. Gabe pulls his arm from his brother's grasp.

"Don't pull my family into this, dumbass," Gabe mumbles.

"Whether you like it or not, they have been involved since the beginning. I've had to watch Anna see you like this. It's hurting them as well as yourself, Gabe. This needs to stop. I know it used to be fun when we were young, but things are different now. Dad is gone and we're all grown up. You need to be responsible for your actions," Andre begs

Gabe hates hearing those words because he knows his brother is right. He knows this is a problem. He's seen it in his wife's eyes everytime he comes home from another job he's lost. How his kids haven't spoken to him for longer than a few minutes because he's never sober enough to make conversation with them. He thinks about how much they will hate him when they're older every day of his life, but he can't stop. If only the pain would, the empty void in his life where his father used to be. He shakes his head and nudges Andre away.

"Leave me alone, for once. I can take care of myself." They both knew that was a lie, but Gabe was too inebriated to care at his point. Andre threw his arms up.

"I don't know what to do with you," Andre proclaims. "I give up; I genuinely give up. You are so fricken stubborn! Just like Dad…"

"Again with the negativity…" Gabe shakes his head. He wanted Andre to leave, to let him sit in his pain and wallow in it, like he always has. It's what he deserves for what he's been through. He's a failure, and he deserves nothing less than a shot of whiskey or something stronger. He'd never admit he's wrong in front of Andre. Andre has always had the better lot in life, even with his own drinking problem.

"I haven't had a drink in six years, not since Dad died, and I don't plan on it. You'd do well to remember what it did to me and what it will do to you if you go on like this." Andre plunges his hands in his pockets, then gives Gabe a short, sarcastic wave. "Take care of yourself...if you can."

"Wasn't that a nice night, though, when we went out together after he died?" Andre stops in his tracks as Gabe's words give him pause.

"Since when do you remember that fondly?" Andre turns slowly.

"Come on, we hadn't spoken for months and then he brought us together again, like he always did." Gabe plays with the shot glass.

"You had insisted I was the one who started that fight and you never admitted you were wrong."

"It was about one dinner! I wanted to pay for your anniversary dinner, but you wouldn't let me!"

"Because it's my day to treat my wife—" Andre stops himself, holding his hands up. "I digress, what is your point?"

"We hadn't been that close since our school days," Gabe reminisces. "Dad was always making sure we could resolve our shit and get along."

"That night contributed to my drinking problem, and you consider it a good night?" Andre rounds on him and turns him in the stool to face him. "And his death eventually led to this, whatever you've become." Andre gestures to all of Gabe.

"We were at peace for at least a little bit of time..." Gabe tries again, but Andre isn't having it. Just as Andre was about to answer, another voice spoke up again.

"Do you kids mind? A man is trying to drink peacefully here." There is that man again, that odd stranger. His tone is more amused than scolding, as if he's enjoying this bickering.

"Do *you* mind?" Gabe counters. Gabe notices Andre staring at the man. "We're having a discussion here, a private one."

"Sounds very private when you're speaking as loudly as you are." The man raises an eyebrow.

"Have we met before?" Andre asks. "You speak like someone familiar."

"I have a way of speaking that is very common." The man shrugs. "I don't know why you'd think that because we've definitely never met. I can guarantee you that."

The man turned and sipped his whiskey.

"Well, if you're done trying to make your terrible point, Gabe, I'm leaving. Have a nice life." Andre throws his hands into the air and walks towards the door.

"Well, that was productive." Gabe sighs and goes to drink from the bottle again, but Doug stops him.

"I give you a glass for a reason." Doug is wearing a hat now and an outdoor coat. "Marisha is on the next shift and she's gonna kick your butt if she sees you doing that...even if you do pay for the whole bottle."

"Fine by me, you heading out now?"

"Can't get out of here faster, but it is great to see you again, man. You should probably listen to your brother." Doug tips his hat and makes his way down the bar.

"If I did, how would you survive without my company?"

"Oh I think I'd do just fine." Doug winks.

"You wound me." Gabe gestures dramatically.

"Goodnight, man." Gabe raises his glass to Doug on his way out and downs it again. Marisha comes down the bar and eyes him. Gabe nods as if he's done nothing wrong.

After a few minutes of silence, listening to the ambiance of the evening chatter, his thoughts went to that night he spent with his brother in this same tavern six years ago. He and Andre were sitting here at the bar with drinks in their hands. They were talking about their father. Andre brought up this one time when Dad tried to dance at his wedding and how it was a big hit. And then Gabe brought up a story where he saw Dad cry after he and their mother had a massive fight. It was the most vulnerable he had ever seen his dad, and it terrified him. If his dad could cry, the bravest person he knew, then the world truly wasn't perfect.

He and Andre had laughed and cried together that night. When the night ended for Gabe, it didn't for Andre. He kept up his drinking and damn near lost him his job, until his wife gave him an ultimatum; get help or get another wife. Andre chose the former and started changing himself.

Gabe glances at the bottle of Jack and realizes he is only halfway through. He's still unable to get rid of that guilty feeling in his chest. Andre coming to see him and chew him out was needed, but it only made Gabe feel worse. His phone rings and it's Anna; his heart beats in his throat. Gabe takes a deep breath and answers it.

"Hey, babe, how's it going?" Gabe is trying his darndest to keep the slur from his voice by speaking as carefully as he can.

"Where are you?" she asks. Her voice is small, and he can tell she's worried.

"Just down the road for a night with the boys," Gabe proclaims.

"You didn't go to work drunk again, did you?" Her tone turns darker.

"Me, do that? No way! We got a full good few clients reviewing us this morning, and now...we're celebrating!" Gabe tries to make the last part sound more exciting, but it almost betrays him. He hears Anna sigh on the other line. She knows him better than anyone. He knows she can tell he's lying, but she won't admit it.

"Well, I'll put the kids to bed and get ready for my shift tomorrow. You make sure you get home safe." She heaves another heavy sigh.

"I'll be fine, only two miles down the road." Gabe fiddles with the glass. "You sleep well, babe. I love you." He waits almost an eternity for her to answer with the sentiment. Part of him thought she would just hang up without saying it back.

"Sure, love you too." And then she hangs up.

Gabe pulls his phone from his ear and glances at his background. A picture of him and his family. It's similar to the one he had in his work station, but it's in a different setting. They are standing under the big bucket at a waterpark that is about to drop water on the four of them. Gabe always found this picture funny because it spells their doom, but they don't even know it yet. He smiles at it and then he stares at Anna. She looks so happy holding their youngest in her arms, looking into his eyes as he does hers. He wishes he could be better to her...be the perfect husband she thought she was getting on the day they got married.

He feels the presence of someone sitting on the stool beside him, the one Andre was sitting on while he was there. He takes a moment to ignore the man before his curiosity takes over his drunken mind.

Gabe looks over and sees the stranger sitting beside him, the one making remarks before. The man takes a sip of his Whiskey and looks over at Gabe.

"Hello, Gabriel," he says. "I think it's time you and I had a chat."

Chapter 3:

Who the Hell Are You?

Gabriel gapes at the man. He doesn't recognize him, nor has he encountered him before in this bar. He is also confused at the image of such a man dressed in that way drinking such a drink.

"Do I know you?"

"In a sense, yes. I should hope so," the man says, sipping his wine.

"That doesn't answer my question. I may not be sober, but I know I've never seen you before." Gabe leans in a little closer to get a better look. "Nah, don't know you."

"You don't? That's a shame. I know you very well, son." The man nodded to him. "Would a stranger know you have a wife and kids? I bet they're doing great these days."

Gabe stopped mid-sip and stared at the man, narrowing his eyes. "Who the hell are you? How do you know me?"

The mysterious man turns to him and smiles with a shrug. "Let's just say, I am who I am."

Gabe shakes his head, pursing his lips. "I have no idea what that means…is that a reference to something?"

"It means that I am. It comes from a book someone wrote about me."

"A book about you? I didn't know famous people knew about this bar…"

"I didn't say I was famous, but I suppose you could say that."

"You never answered my question. Who are you?"

"Who I am."

"Okay, now you've lost me. I need another drink for this." Gabe holds his hand up in defeat and pours another shot, drinking it down heavily.

"I am who I am. The being of beings. The creator of all existence, etcetera etcetera. I am God." The man raises his arms as if to gesture to himself, raising an eyebrow, as if it were obvious, or should have been obvious.

Gabe spits out the last of his shot, covering a bit of the bar in front of him in whiskey. He wipes it up quickly, glances from the man, back to the bottle, barstool, and shakes his head. "This must finally be hitting me hard. I just thought I heard you say you're God." Gabe snickers. "That would be crazy…"

"That's what I'm saying. I am the being who you guys would know as God." The man nods and downs the final bit of his drink.

"You say you're 'God.' Prove it then." Gabe turns to the man and crosses his arms.

The man calling himself God holds up his glass and places it a little closer between him and Gabe. He keeps his eyes on Gabe as Gabe stares at the glass, confused. It instantly fills up with whiskey as if being poured from an invisible source, out of thin air. Gabe's eyes are wide.

"What—how did you do that? Is that some kind of magic trick? Is there some hose you're hiding?" Gabe is looking beneath the bar and behind God to figure out where the whiskey came from. "What are you, some kind of magician?"

"I am God. It was empty and I filled it. That's the least of what I can do." The man smiles and leans closer to him, raising an eyebrow. "Need more convincing?"

God rises from his barstool and stands in place. He holds his hands out, and slowly his body levitates from the ground. He is floating there in a solid-state as if he were standing on an invisible platform.

Gabe has had enough. "No way, I'm done with this. There is not enough alcohol in the world…"

Gabe gets up from his stool and stumbles into a chair at another table. He falls to the ground in a daze. He finds himself looking back at the levitating "God" and gets up slowly, rushing towards the door as fast as his drunken brain will allow his legs to move. He finally makes it to the door and he opens it, but he stops just as he is about to run through. The door does not lead to the parking lot, but the same room he's in. The same floor, bar, stools, and tables are all mirrored through the door he assumed is an exit. He closes the door and turns to see God behind him. Gabe cowers against the door and covers his eyes.

"Please don't hurt me...whoever you are!" Gabe shouts. He can see a small glow of light through his fingers. He uncovers his eyes to see God standing over him. He is glowing in a heavenly light that can't easily be described. It is bright but not blinding, yet soft and warm like a hug from a loved one. Gabe looks around and notices that no one else has reacted to the commotion, nor the glow emanating from the man standing in front of him. God kneels on one knee and holds a hand out to Gabe.

"Come, bud, we have a lot to talk about," God says with a warm smile. Gabe snaps out of his awe of the glow and the man before him and takes the hand held out to him. God pulls him up slowly and without difficulty. They both walk back to their stools, and God gestures for Gabe to sit first before taking his seat. God takes a sip of his wine. "I'm sorry to frighten you like that, but you did ask for proof."

"Yes. Yes, I did. I'm still not sure if I regret it or not."

"I sure hope not. I had to convince you it was really me, in whatever way I could."

Gabe nods. "I can understand that. You're not what I expected..."

"No, I suppose I'm not Morgan Freeman, though I do think that is one of my favorite portrayals."

Gabe is confused. He knows what is happening now; God is really here, sitting in this bar with him, but it still takes a bit for him to wrap his head around the concept. He has so many questions and is unsure of how to ask them.

"I'll give you a few minutes to take all this in. Please take your time. I don't do this often, but I do at least understand how you're feeling."

"I have so many questions…"

"I am here before you to answer them." God smiles warmly. "Take all the time you need."

"Give me just one second…" Gabe holds his hand up with his finger pointed upwards.

"Of course." God nods, still smiling.

"Great." Gabe almost falls off the stool as he rushes to the little boy's room. He bursts through the door and almost falls again as he reaches the sink.

Gabe splashes some water on his face and dries himself off with a paper towel. He looks up at himself in the mirror.

"God is out there. Sitting on that stool." Gabe is amazed at the words coming out of his mouth. "Holy crap, God is sitting on that stool."

He shakes his head slowly and glances down at the sink and then back up at the mirror.

"I snapped and yelled at God when he was eavesdropping…" Gabe has a wave of realization.

Just as he's about to say another thing, a toilet flushes. He freezes, realizing someone just heard him and bolts from the bathroom. He hides behind the corner, looking around the bar, seeing God still sitting there.

"There's no chance, if you're hoping I'll leave." God appears to be talking to himself, but he looks in Gabe's direction. Gabe can't move. He's frozen to the spot. *How does he do that?* he asks himself, and then remembers. *Oh yeah, he's God.*

"Come join me when you're ready." God holds up his drink in a toasting manner and nods to Gabe across the room.

He turns and hides behind the wall leading to the restroom. He looks around the bar and sees no one else has noticed the exchange. No one else has seen that God was talking to himself; to him.

After what felt like an eternity, Gabe waltzes back to the stool beside God as if he means to, as if he had never left.

God turns to face him, leaning his arm on the bar and regarding Gabe. His posture is slouched, natural for the body he's using, but he still holds a regal aura to his presence. God was sitting beside him, relatable but yet not human. Gabe couldn't explain it, but that's what he's seeing at this moment. God speaks slowly and carefully, like one would to a child who needs to have it explained to him that monsters don't live under his bed.

"Gabriel, you don't need to be afraid," he says. "I am not here to harm you, or 'smite' you, or anything. As I said, I am only here to talk with you. Think of this like sitting down to have a drink with an old friend or relative. No need for formalities, of course."

Gabe takes a moment to think about it and then nods. "Okay, I'll do that," he says. "I'm sorry about before...when I was rude to you."

God waves his hand dismissively. "Oh, no harm done. I was just listening in, and I bet I should have been more discreet. I couldn't resist a little bit of eavesdropping." God winked at him.

"You cheeky bastard." Gabe covers his mouth. "I just called God a cheeky bastard…"

God laughs heartily. "It's all right!" He claps Gabe on the back, nearly winding him. "It's refreshing."

"Either way, that is stopping right now. I'm done."

"Perfect." God sips his whiskey. "Now, take your time, and ask me anything you'd like."

Well, here goes nothing...

Chapter 4:

So...I Got Some

Questions...

Gabe has taken a few minutes to collect his thoughts and drink some water to sober himself up a little more. Hopefully, his brain can work a little more coherently. He still couldn't believe he was sitting here, in a bar, with the Almighty, God, the big man in the sky.

"No offense, but you don't really look like what I would imagine if I met God."

God smiles and shrugs. "I don't come down here to get noticed."

"Fair enough, I guess." Gabe nods. "I can't lie and say I don't have a million questions for you."

"Whether it's a million or not, I'm here to listen." God strokes his beard thoughtfully. "I do have all night."

"Okay, you ready?"

"I'm God."

"Right…" Gabe shakes his head and waves his finger. "That's a good one."

"I am the master of what my children have begun to call dad jokes."

"You are the…big daddy, as it were." Gabe frowned. "That felt dirty coming out of my mouth…"

God laughs, a big, booming laugh like a sailor. "All jokes aside, ask away, bud."

Gabe clears his throat and gets straight to the point. "Why are you here? It's not like I'm super religious, so why me?"

"You are human right?"

"I mean, yes, last I checked." Gabe shrugs, glancing down at himself. "My question stands, though."

God shrugs as if it's simple. "It was time we talked. You're at the lowest point in your life, and like it or not, believe in me or not, you are still my child."

"Right, of course. All that, 'we are all your children' stuff." Gabe makes quotations with his fingers. Then he realizes to whom he's speaking. "Sorry…a force of habit."

"No worries, of course." God winks. "Another?"

"If you are the one pulling the strings, this 'Big Plan,' then why did you do all this to me? Why did I have to get busted?"

God snickers and sips his whiskey. "Hey kid, it's not my fault you showed up to work drunk."

"Hard blow…but you have a point." Gabe faces forward and gazes at the wall. "I never thought I would ever hear God call me 'bro'…"

"You can't be finished yet…"

"Well, in that case, why won't you stop me from making bad decisions?" Gabe is distressed now and angry at himself. God places a hand on his shoulder. "How could you let me go this low and screw up my life this badly?"

"Free will, bud. You make the decision, you live with the consequences."

Gabe holds his own hands out. "Then why are there bad consequences? Isn't this supposed to be a perfect world you created for us to live in?"

"Bro, I did. I literally created a perfect garden for you guys and you got tricked by a sausage tube with teeth."

"Wait what?! Did it really happen like that?!" Gabe gapes at him.

"No, the garden was real, but you guys were miserable there. You, as my creations, were unique in that you had a soul, but the soul needs challenges and strife to grow. Without it, you became content, then bored. And with nothing to challenge you, it turned into misery. Because there would never be a challenge from which you could grow, you all grew hopeless. It broke my heart, but I had to let you guys into a world where I knew you would feel pain, but without the pain, you had no frame of reference for happiness."

Gabe blinks and nods. "That's really...profound...bro."

Yep. He did it. He called God "bro." Gabe could almost hear Anna poking fun at him.

"Thank you." God nods.

"Do you feel emotions?" Gabe asks. "I'll be honest, I always had this image where you were just this stoic being in the sky."

"Oh yeah, I feel feelings. I created you all in my image. I didn't give you *all* of my emotions because you wouldn't be able to handle them. But yes, I feel." God looks away and sighs. "I feel a lot."

Gabe hesitates to continue. "Do you need a minute?"

"No, keep going, this is entertaining." God smiles.

"How do you feel about atheists?"

God shrugs and sits back, leaning one arm on the bar as he faces Gabe again. "I want to say I didn't expect that question, but it's inevitable. The answer to that is that I do honestly love them."

"You're telling me you love those who don't believe and are sometimes even against your existence?" Gabe stares at him.

"Look, bud, I created the universe and the science it runs on. Even though they don't believe in me, it's nice that they at least appreciate my work enough to try to figure out how it works. And at the end of the day, they're my children too. I like them a lot actually, they bring the most unique perspectives into the world that sometimes go unnoticed."

"What about homosexuals?" Gabe asks.

"Gabriel, they're my children and I love them. Choosing the person you love, even if society or others tell you it's wrong, is the ultimate form of free will. The greatest gift I ever gave you all was the ability to love someone else." God looks Gabe in the eye. "No matter what people say, I accept them. Case closed."

"I thought so, but you know—" Gabe waves his hands in a gesture, trying to find an answer.

"You had to ask, I understand," God remarks, sipping his whiskey. "It's always been a debate, and I wish you could all see them how I do. The wonderful people they are and the most expressive humans I know."

"So, do you ever help heal anyone from disease? When a devout person says they've been healed after surviving cancer, and thanking you, did you actually do it?" Gabe leans closer in anticipation.

"No, of course not." God shakes his head. "I haven't intervened for a long time. I had to stop or else things would flow the same way as in the garden. Sausage tube and all."

"But why not?"

"Because you must be left to figure it out on your own." God taps the bar counter with two of his fingers to emphasize his point. "If I came around and cured every disease on the planet, it would be too easy. Everyone would be too reliant on me for their problems, and some of them already are when there's nothing I did for them."

"Wow, I think I learned something today."

"I sure hope you did, man. Not many people get the opportunity to meet me and tell the tale."

"Wait, what—?"

"Everyone who meets me is dead. Usually. You're not."

"Great." Gabe nods awkwardly. "I'm speaking to God, in a bar, and I'm not dead."

Gabe was very grateful for that fact. Being alive does suck, but dying would suck more.

"So, what do we do now?"

"I'm here to talk with you, Gabriel. I have a feeling we've just touched the surface." God winks.

"We have been talking," Gabe says. "What should we talk about?"

"I don't know, I assume you have more questions for me."

"Oh, you have no idea…"

"You can ask me anything you like; we have all night."

"This is so weird, I said I grew up Catholic, but I suddenly grew out of it," Gabe explains. "I just didn't feel like it was for me anymore. No offense…"

"None was taken at all." God shrugs. "You can relax, you know. I'm not going to do anything to you. Least of all for not believing in me for so long."

"Oh thank god…sorry."

"It's okay; contrary to popular belief, I don't mind when people say my name in vain," God says. "I find it gives you all some personality when you do that."

"I hope you know this is weird for me, and I will definitely be apologizing every time I say that." Gabe holds his hands up.

"I understand completely. I would be more confused if you had expected me here." God snickers.

"Haha, imagine that." Gabe laughs uncomfortably.

"Ah, come on." God wraps his arm around Gabe's neck in a friendly gesture. "I'm God, your creator; in all literal senses of the word, you are my son. Let's have a good time tonight. In whatever way will make you feel comfortable."

"About that…" Gabe mutters.

Chapter 5:

Shots?

Gabe isn't sure what to do in this situation. Nor is he sure how he feels. He's still struggling to take this all in. He looks around the bar, and there's nothing out of the ordinary, other than his inability to leave the bar. God was patient in the silence between them. It wasn't as awkward as it should be. The chatter of the bar around them was minimal but present. Gabe closed his eyes and sighed. He glanced at the whiskey bottle. He holds it up and nods to it.

"Let me buy you a shot," Gabe offers. "Or maybe, a few shots…"

"Sure, son. Why not?" God winks.

Gabe calls the bartender and orders some shots. A thought comes to Gabe's mind, and he says it out loud. "Can you even get drunk?"

God shrugs. "I can do whatever I want, bud. I'm God."

"You like whiskey I take it?"

"Sure do, and my glass is getting a little dry, so grab some." God gestures behind him. Gabe looks around for Marisha, the bartender for the night, but she's nowhere to be found.

"Where is she?" Gabe asks.

God snickers. "It's all good, man, just go get it."

"Free bar?" Gabe looks around.

"Free bar. My treat, bud. No funny business, though."

Gabe stands still for a moment, reveling in the implications if he disobeys God...*the* God.

"Nope, not at all." Gabe shakes his head. He goes behind the bar and looks around, finding the most expensive whiskey available. He brings it to their glasses and pours two shots from the other side of the bar.

"To everlasting life." God holds up his shot in a toast. Gabe snickers. God laughs along with him. "Couldn't resist."

"Eh, why not. To everlasting life." Gabe holds up his shot in the same gesture, and their glasses make a satisfying *clang* sound as they touch. Gabe and God both down the shots. Gabe takes it worse than God does. Gabe lets out a couple of coughs. "Wow, this shit is strong. Oh god, I just swore...wow, I'm sorry. Dang, it…"

God laughs a loud hearty laugh.

"Out of politeness, I'll try not to."

"You do you, kid." God shrugs and leans against the bar.

"Care for another shot?"

"Can you handle it?" God looks a little concerned, stroking his beard.

Gabe nods and leans closer. "Bring it on, God."

Gabe keeps eye contact with the Almighty and pours the shots. He downs the shot, this time trying his best to keep in the coughing fit the whiskey provokes in his throat.

"Wow." Gabe lets a few coughs escape as he tries to speak. "This is godly stuff." Gabe winks at the man in front of him on the other side of the bar.

"That's a good one!" God laughs.

"This is pretty fun, drinking with God," Gabe reflects.

"If you could hold your shots, it might be even more fun." God winks again. Gabe rolls his eyes.

"Now you really sound like you're my dad. I mean, I guess you are, but my dad used to make jokes like that."

"I've heard so much about you from him." God smiles.

Gabe shakes his head, intending to avoid those thoughts. "What shall we do now…?"

"Another shot?"

"Yes, but what after…" Gabe thinks for a moment. He looks around the bar where people are sitting at tables and playing darts. Gabe shrugs. "Hey, I'm not too bad at darts."

"Are you challenging me to a game of darts?" God raises his eyebrows. "You really don't get the whole God thing, do you?"

Gabe holds his arms out in a shrug. "Hey, even if I lose, there's no shame. But honestly, who else can say they've played a game of darts with God?"

God purses his lips and nods in approval. "Fair enough, let's play."

God and Gabe toast their shots once again, clink the glasses, and drink them down before moving to the dartboard.

Gabe honestly can't remember the last time he played darts. He knows he's not going to be a pro, but he wants to try. It's his turn first. He throws his three shots and hits the bull's eye once. God nods.

"Impressive for a man who's constantly drunk." He claps Gabe on the shoulder. Gabe rolls his eyes as he walks to the board to pull out his darts.

"Just shoot your shots." Gabe crosses his arms and watches. God gets all three bull's eyes in a row. God looks back at him and smiles, pulling his darts from the board.

"Beginner's luck?" God winks.

After a few games of darts, where God kicks Gabe's butt, Gabe wins at least one game.

"Tenth time's the charm!" Gabe pulls his darts from the board. "You let me win, didn't you?"

"I was kicking your butt too hard. I had to at least once."

"I never thought God would be so competitive..." Gabe nods.

"I can be whatever I want to be. I have high standards for myself."

"I expect nothing less, my man." Gabe points a finger gun at God and then sighs.

"What next?"

"How about some card games?"

"What card games are we talking about?"

Gabe walks behind the bar and pulls out a deck of Uno cards. He was confident he would be able to outsmart God, if only just once.

"Ever played Uno?"

"A couple of times. I saw when it came out and was curious enough to see what the fuss was about." God nods to him. "Bring it on."

The game goes well for Gabe, at first. But he is playing Uno with God, of all beings. Just when Gabe thinks he has the upper hand, God goes and throws him for a loop, adding a "Draw 4" card to the pile every so often, more than Gabe can keep up. Gabe sighs as his thoughts drift to why he came here. God notices this without seeing it and points it out.

"What's with the sigh?" God says, looking up from behind his hand of cards. Gabe shakes his head, a little nervous that God noticed him being vulnerable, but he leans into it.

"Must be the alcohol making me think too much," Gabe says.

"It's supposed to make you think less, as I recall, but you should know well enough how emotional it makes you feel." God looks up at him with the eyes of a concerned father. "Is this reminding you of something?"

"No, I was thinking about my grandparents." Gabe takes a deep breath as the images of his grandparents emerge into his thoughts. "Things were easier back when I was younger. I would go to their house almost every weekend when my mom and I went to visit them. I would even sometimes stay with them, and they would take me to school if my mom worked early shifts."

God and Gabe laughed. "She sounds like a wonderful lady."

"Oh, my grandma was. She used to own a tavern similar to this one, but it's not around anymore." Gabe tries to leave it at that.

"I remember meeting them. They are wonderful souls."

"Yeah, yeah, they were." Gabe looks down at his cards again. As they play, he notices that people are indeed entering through the door, but no one has been leaving. It's an odd thing, but normal for the bar at this late hour. He feels God looking at him, probably hoping he would say more, but Gabe is still trying to avoid vulnerability. It's safer that way.

"What's your favorite memory of them?"

"What?"

"Your grandparents, what's your favorite memory from when they were alive?"

Gabe thinks for a moment, staring at his cards but not really looking at them. He had so many to choose from. He picked the first one he could think of.

"There was this one time when I was a child…"

God leans closer, interested.

"You know this one?"

"I will once you continue."

"Right, well, I was bullied a lot as a kid, right?" Gabe begins. "There was this one time I was being chased and ran to the tavern rather than home."

Gabe suddenly finds himself standing in the parking lot of his middle school, God at his side. Gabe jumps at the sight of him. "What the hell? How are we here?"

"God magic, of course. I took us back to the memory. Think of this like *The Christmas Carol*, and you're Scrooge."

"Hey, I may be a drunk, but I'm no Scrooge."

"Look, there they are." God points his index finger in the direction of a few boys that are running towards 10-year-old Gabe.

"Hey, there's the nerd! Get him!" their leader, Tommy, shouts.

Gabe hears them behind him and runs as fast as he can. The kids catch up to him when he trips. They kick him a few times. Gabe lies there crying.

"Stop, please!"

"What, you gonna call your mommy?" another kid says.

Gabe sees an opportunity and pulls on the legs on one of the guys, causing him to trip. A yelling teacher makes the boys stop. Gabe gets up and bolts away as fast as he can. The other boys and Tommy chase after him again. Gabe runs and runs until he can see his grandparents' tavern down the road. He makes it there and tries to open the heavy door, but the kids make it to him first. They knock him down and he screams again.

"Hey! You kids leave him alone!" Grandma's voice is a welcome sound to Gabe's ears. The kids stop hurting him and he rushes to Grandma. The kids laugh.

"Look at this runt, needs his granny to help him." Tommy points and laughs as the other kids follow suit.

Grandma pulls Gabe behind her and she walks up to them. "You kids should be ashamed of yourselves, kicking a kid while he's down," she scolds them. "That makes you cowards."

"B-but, he hit us first!" Tommy points in Gabe's direction.

"And that means you can hit him back?"

"Yeah, I guess—" Tommy is cut off by Grandma slapping him across the face. Gabe was caught off guard by the gesture, and his mouth hangs open. It wasn't a hard slap, but enough to make a sound.

"Now you know how it feels." Grandma squats down to the child's level. "Are you going to hit me now?"

Tommy rubs his cheek and begins to tear up. He pushes through his friends and runs away sobbing. "My mommy's gonna hear about this!"

"You tell her!" Grandma calls after them. "I'll tell her everything! Mark my words, Tommy boy!" Grandma turns and walks back towards Gabe. "Are you alright, sweetie?"

"You slapped him. Mommy tells me adults shouldn't hit children." Gabe begins to sob. All the emotions from what happened flood out.

"Whenever Grandma's around, no one's touching 'Booger Butt.'"

Gabe pouts. "I'm not a booger butt."

"Yes you are." Grandma messes with Gabe's hair and kisses him on the cheek a few times, making him giggle. "You wanna know why?"

"Why, Granny?"

"Because you're my Booger Butt." She messes with his hair one more time. "Don't tell your momma about this, okay?"

"Okay." Gabe smiles.

"Come on, kid. I'll get you a soda from the tap." Grandma holds her hand out for Gabe to take.

"Yay, soda!" Gabe cheers. He grasps his grandmother's hand and follows her into the tavern.

A few hours later, Gabe's mother bursts into the tavern and rushes to the bar where Gabe is sitting.

"Oh my god, baby, there you are!" She pulls him into her arms and holds him tight.

"He ran straight here after school, some kids chasing after him. I told him he could stay here for a while."

"You could have called me, Mom!"

"I tried, you were busy." Grandma shrugs. "He's fine."

"And full of sugar." Gabe's mom sighs.

"Better than him crying and being sad." Grandma comes around the bar and places her hands on his hips.

"You have a point, I guess…" Gabe's mom considers that. "Okay, bud, let's get home. I have a nice dinner planned for when Daddy gets home. Do you want to help me?"

"Yeah!" Gabe holds a hand up and says the word with the straw still in his mouth. He slurps back the rest of the soda and rushes to hug Grandma. "Thanks for the soda, Granny!"

"Any time, kid," Granny whispers in his ear. "Remember our little secret?"

"Yes, Granny!" Gabe whispers back. She lets him go, and he runs off, waving as he and his mom leave.

Gabe blinks and then finds himself back at the bar. God is sitting beside him just like before. "That was her nickname for me, Booger Butt. She made me feel invincible."

"She's a badass lady," God remarks.

"I remember my mom did end up finding out about the incident." Gabe finds himself smiling. "She got *so* mad at Grandma not even a few days later. The kid's mom came to her and told her what happened." Gabe laughs at the memory.

"Do you miss them?" God asks.

Gabe doesn't look up from his cards, realizing only now the vulnerability he just showed. *So much for being safe…*

"All the time." Gabe places another card down. "Pick up two."

"Pick up four." God places his card down.

Gabe narrows his eyes at God, who's grinning confidently. He knows what he must do, but he lacks the courage. Should he place his next 'pick up two' card, or should he give in? Gabe isn't one to give up, not in these games.

"I play you; pick up six." Gabe smiles again. "I bet you don't…"

God places another card down. "Pick up 8."

Gabe groans. "Goddammit…" He catches himself again. "Sorry."

God snickers. "You get pretty passionate about these games, aren't you?"

"I see you are as well," Gabe counters as he begrudgingly picks up 8 cards.

"I don't get to play it much. I don't think I've played it since it was invented. Hands down one of the best card games you guys ever came up with."

"I can tell you played it a lot back then." Gabe nods to the cards.

"It's not one I can easily forget."

"What other games do you love that humans invented?"

"Hmm, that's a tough one. Solitaire is a favorite. I can always play that alone somewhere and observe some of my children and see how they're doing. Chess as well. I love coming down and playing chess with my children. Hey, would you want to play that?"

"I don't think they do that at this bar," Gabe lies.

"That's crap and you know it, kid." God smirks.

"You've kicked my ass in my favorite game five times now."

"About to make it to six." God places his last card and wins the game.

"This game was always more fun with more people." Gabe sighs and drops his cards on the table. He looks up at God. Gabe remembers that there is a chess set here in this bar. God wasn't wrong, but he hesitates. "Ah screw it, let's play some chess."

"I don't guarantee I'll go easy on you." God gets up from the chair and helps to pack up the cards. Gabe gathers up the cards from God and puts them back in the box. He walks towards the game wall, puts the cards back, then grabs the chess board.

"Oh, I'm going to regret this…" Gabe mutters.

"What was that?" God asks.

"Nothing, just preparing to kick your butt."

"Bring it on, big guy!"

Gabe sets up the board. "So, what do you like about chess?"

God thinks for a moment and shrugs. "I love the strategy of it, the story of war put into a turn-based board game. You have to think so much about your moves, and if you're not careful, you could lose it all. It's a lot of fun!"

Gabe gives God a look of surprise. "Okay, that sounds pretty sadistic, for God, I mean."

"Actually, I think of chess kind of like human lives," God says, making his first move. Gabe makes his own move after a bit of consideration, and looks up at God with a little bit of confusion in his eyes.

"I don't follow...is that a God thing?" Gabe squints as if staring at God will give him the answers he's looking for.

"Sorry, I don't mean to alarm you or weird you out; I just think that it's similar." God makes his next move. "Think of it this way; humans go through life with many twists and turns, making this decision and that, all leading to…" Gabe makes another move and then God traps him. "Checkmate. And that can be heaven, living your dream, anything. It's all up to interpretation."

Gabe heard all of that, but he is staring at the board, dumbfounded. He wonders how God could have won so fast. "How…"

"You wanted to play chess with God." God shrugs. "Can't say I didn't warn ya."

Gabe sets the board up again.

"Want to play again already?" God raises an eyebrow.

"This time, could you go a little easier on me? This game isn't my strong suit, but they don't have a lot here."

"I can do that for you, bud. Who taught you to play?"

"My mom. My dad was more of a hands-on person, and my mom liked games that make you think. I learned, but never stuck with it," Gabe explains. "When I was a teenager, I lost interest, as most teenagers do in most things they liked as children."

"Did you ever play it again?"

"I think this is the first time since I was younger, but it's something that you don't really lose, right?"

God nods. "Yeah, I suppose not." God makes his first move as the winner of the previous game, beginning the current one. As they play, God gives Gabe a fighting chance, of which Gabe is grateful for. Sometimes, it isn't as fun when the one who is challenging you as a player goes easy on you, but in this case, Gabe was fine with it. He's competitive, but not enough to not have a chance to win at all. God takes a glance at him and speaks. "What's your mother like?"

Gabe is quiet for a second, still thinking about making his next move. God has him in Check, so he needs to get out of it. He finally moves his knight towards God's bishop and claims it. Gabe sighs in relief.

"Sorry, I didn't hear that." Gabe looks up again. "What did you say?"

"I asked about your mother; what is she like?"

Gabe nods. "Ah, okay. Well, she's amazing. She and my dad met at her sister's wedding. They didn't get along all the time, but they were devoted to each other until the end. She was always making sure he was in check. If you ask me, she was always the pants in the relationship." Gabe laughs.

God raises an eyebrow again and chuckles. "Really, she's a strong lady."

"Takes after her mother, as you saw in the memory. She didn't always approve of her mother's methods with me, but I think she realizes now that it was better for me than it was worse." Gabe shrugs.

God and Gabe go through a few more moves before God wins again. God shrugs. "Best two out of three?"

Chapter 6:

God's Eye View

After God kicks his ass for the seventh time in Chess, Gabe and God go back to sit at the bar.

"I need a drink after that defeat." Gabe pours himself a shot.

"I need one to celebrate that victory." God winks and sits down on his stool.

"Could have gone a little easy on me."

"You could have been a little better at the game?"

God and Gabe burst into laughter. Gabe pours a shot for God as well. They clink their glasses together and drink them. Gabe almost gags again, but he takes the shot even better this time. Gabe takes a deep breath.

"So, what's it like being God?" he asks.

God shrugs. "That's a loaded question; gotta be more specific, bud."

Gabe internally agrees. He stops and thinks for a moment, then comes back with the question again. "I mean, how does it feel to be the creator of everything?"

God takes a minute to think about the question. Gabe knows it's a big one; it was hard enough to buck up the courage to ask.

"Well, it's hard to explain, Gabe." God strokes his beard and leans on the back of the stool. "You know, in the beginning, it was just me, and I was alone for a long time before anything in the universe was created."

"That must have been pretty lonely." Gabe leans forward on the bar, watching God as he explains.

"It was, but I had a lot of time to think, to build this idea in my head." God waves his hands around as he explains the next bit. "It's hard for you to imagine this, of course, because your lives are so short, but I remember creating matter and watching it explode and expand across the void. It truly was a beautiful sight."

"I bet it was," Gabe interjected. "Going from nothing to a vast universe in seconds must have been the greatest thing you'd ever see."

"It was indeed, but not quite the greatest; that title goes to watching you all grow." God shakes a finger in the air as if he was scolding someone. "I vividly remember when I saw it, that floating ball of magma swirling and forming, all the while knowing that humans would walk on that planet one day."

Gabe could see God smiling, his eyes seeming to glaze over like tears were forming. "I'll never forget the pride I had when you guys figured out how to create a reading and writing system. How you guys learned to build homes instead of just living in caves." God stops for a moment, shaking his head solemnly.

Gabe nods. "I think I have an idea of what you mean."

"Yes, it's similar to how you felt when Kayla first learned to ride a bike," God explains as Gabe looks away, bringing back that memory.

"She was so nervous, she didn't want me to let go," Gabe reminisces.

"That's exactly how I felt." God sighs. "It was hard to let you all go and let you be your own people. You know, I've watched you guys not only develop as individuals, but also as a group. All of you have done such wonderful things."

"Humans are good at adapting, I'll give us that," Gabe says.

"You went from nothing to a burst of something, kind of like the universe." God crosses his arms as he continues to speak. "I was fascinated to see the surge in the evolution of technology over the last couple of centuries. Some things I hadn't even thought you all would think of. Electricity, handheld computers, airplanes, the Internet." God shakes his head proudly, and then his gaze centers on Gabe. "Even watching your family tree grow and thrive, with all the good and the bad. You and your wife, raising your children. It's been a pleasure watching you build your life with Anna. How about we revisit that first building block you both started?"

Gabe glances at God and is confused. "When me and Anna got married?"

"After that." God nudges him. "When Kayla was born!"

Gabe again finds himself in another setting with God standing beside him as they observe the scene. They're in a hospital this time. He sees himself and Anna in the room, having a conversation.

"So, who do you think she's going to look like the most?" Gabe asks, glancing at her from the chair.

Anna lay in the hospital bed, rubbing her swollen stomach.

"I mean, of course she'll look like me." Anna side-eyes him with a smile.

"Hey, how would you know?"

"It's, like, a thing where the first born daughters look like the mom and the sons look like the father," Anna says. "Which means, she's gonna look like me—Oh man that was a big one…"

"Want me to call the nurse?" Gabe is frantic.

"Yeah, she's ready…" Anna nods vigorously.

"I was scared to death," Gabe admits to God as they follow the gurney to the delivery room.

"How so? Your generation of people has had *vastly* less deaths from childbirth than in other centuries," God points out.

"That's not why I was nervous." Gabe shakes his head.

"Ahh, for being a father?" God nods a few times. "Yes, that is a nerve-wracking experience."

"I was terrified to meet her, yet so excited at the same time. I was almost as nervous as I was at my wedding, but it was dialed up to eleven."

God and Gabe watch as Anna goes into labor.

"Don't worry, I'm right here, keep going!" Gabe holds Anna's hand as she squeezes his.

"I am going!" Anna yells.

After a lot of screaming and pushing, Anna and Gabe hear the crying of a newborn, their daughter. Anna begins to cry, and so does Gabe. He kisses her forehead.

"I'm so proud of you," he says. "I love you."

"I love you too," Anna pants as she sobs. The doctors check on their new baby girl, then wrap her up and hand her to Anna.

"Hey there, Kayla, welcome to the world," Anna says quietly with a tired voice.

"She's so beautiful; I wonder where she gets it from." Gabe smiles at his wife and kisses her again.

Gabe thinks about Anna and everything he's done to her since he started drinking a lot more. She always had such promising goals for them and their family. To go traveling, move somewhere nice, even just have a good college fund for their children. He shakes the thoughts out of his head.

"You okay, Gabe?" God glances over at him.

"Yeah, just thinking too much again." Gabe shakes his head again and smiles as he watches him and Anna admire Kayla.

"That's never good." God furrows his brow. Gabe is grateful that he takes the hint again and doesn't push it further. God has brought Gabe back to the bar.

"That was one of the greatest moments of my life," Gabe admits. "Seeing my daughter there, finally being able to meet her; it was like heaven."

"Not exactly, but it does come close." God nods.

Gabe comes back to himself and realizes what he said. "Yeah, that's what I meant... How about the dinosaurs?" Gabe asks. "What was it like watching them on earth before we took over?"

"It was more of an experiment." God leans against the bar again, this time propping his chin on his hand. "I knew I would have humans inherit the earth, but I wanted to see how it would fair with only animals populating the planet rather than highly intelligent beings such as yourselves."

"How did it go?"

"Many generations, as you might know, but it was their time." God looks a little sad. "I knew it was time to see your species' ancestors evolve into what you became. I was sad to see them go, but it's also been a pleasure to see humans studying them and trying to figure out what they looked like."

"Sounds like you wanted to see if those dinos could soar." Gabe shoots finger guns at God. He laughs at the bad joke. "I can't believe you find that funny."

"Even I, the Father of all, can find a dad joke hilarious." God chuckles. "I created them, of course."

"Seriously, though, any chance you'll tell me what they *actually* looked like?" Gabe leans in. "The dinosaurs?"

God looks him in the eye with a wry smile. "Nice try, son; not a chance. That's for me to know and humans to figure out."

"Damn, so close!" Gabe shakes his fist at the ceiling. "I guess we'll never know."

"I did see some dinosaur age animals continue to exist." God crosses his arms again, raising an eyebrow.

"Yeah, I know of a few."

"The resilience of life always amazes me." God glances at Gabe. "I have also enjoyed watching you grow up and thrive."

"I'm hardly thriving now."

"You had your moments." God ponders for a few minutes, stroking his beard. "Let's see, what about this one?"

And Gabe finds himself taken back to the memory. It's as if it was a dream. He's watching himself standing in a cheap suit.

"What is this?" Gabe mutters.

"Your wedding day; don't you remember?" God appears beside him, and Gabe nearly jumps out of his skin. "Oh sorry, son, didn't mean to scare you."

"Jeez, you need to warn me when you do this…"

"Sorry, son, I'll prepare you for next time."

"You nearly gave me a—"

"Shh, here's when you see her dress." God nudges him and points.

Gabe followed his pointing finger and watched as Anna came up behind his past self. Gabe was captivated just watching her. The memory of how he felt seeing her for the first time was mirrored in the look on his younger face. Eyes wide and filled with tears as he knew that she was going to be his wife. This beautiful, smart, cunning woman would be his partner for life.

"She looked so beautiful; I cried on the spot." Gabe chuckles to himself, tears falling from his eyes. He realizes this and wipes a few away with his sleeve. God pulls Gabe to follow as they walk to the wedding ceremony. It was a small ceremony in the church his parents used to take him and Andre to when they were children. He almost feels he could see through the eyes of his past self as he watched the scene play out from his point of view.

He's walking down the aisle now that all his groomsmen, along with Andre as his best man, and Anna's sister as her maid of honor, are in their places. He watches as he feels what his younger self is feeling, with bated breath, waiting for his bride. Anna glides down the aisle like an angel in human form, her dress moving with her and her train behind her like a sea of white lighting her path. Gabe watches as she approaches him with her father by her side. The ceremony goes on, and Gabe finds himself especially choked up when they say their vows.

"Anna, I promise to be there for you, and always be your best friend. When I met you, you set my heart on fire. Literally, you blew up our science experiment in sophomore year and my shirt was singed." That got a laugh from the guests. "It's fitting, of course, because my heart was on fire for you from then on. You are my light in the dark and my humor when I am sad. I promise to be the same to you and more. Bring you light when your thoughts are dark, and a bad joke when you need to smile. Or even simply a stiff drink. I can't wait to spend my life with you building up our life together. I love you."

Gabe bows his head, and he feels God's eyes on him. As the emotions flow through him, he finally looks up as he watches his younger self kiss the bride.

He closes his eyes, and when he opens them, he is back in the bar, sitting on the stool. God is sitting by his side like he has been this whole night.

Gabe takes a deep breath. "I promised her the world and beyond. To be the best husband and father and whatever she needed," Gabe mutters to himself as he bows his head again and sighs, wiping the tears away.

"You have been." God places a hand on his shoulder. "Don't sell yourself too short. Here, let this memory cheer you up. This is also a favorite of mine."

Gabe blinks and he is standing in the schoolyard of his high school. God is beside him again and still makes him jump. God snickers and points.

"There you are, sixteen years old," God says.

"This is before I met Anna. There's Andre with those boys in the corner there." Gabe points at them. He and God walk closer as Andre is being pushed by the boys he's in the corner with. Teenage Gabe hears the commotion and rushes to push the boys off his brother.

"Don't you have other things to do? Like, I don't know, go fuck each other's moms or something?" he says.

Gabe visibly cringes as he hears himself say that. God snickers.

"Kids, amiright?…" Gabe mutters, covering his face.

The bullies include Tommy and his cronies.

"Those are the same kids from your middle school memory," God points out.

"Yes, they are…" Gabe admits, crossing his arms.

The kids all laugh at Gabe and Andre. Gabe helps his brother up and punches the closest kid. A fight ensues where Andre and Gabe continuously throw punches at the bullies.

"I remember this fight. It was the first time we'd been suspended as a duo." Gabe crosses his arms and nods.

"Hey! Break it up, kids!" A female teacher rushes up. The other kids rush off scared, leaving Andre and Gabe to be taken to the office.

"No fighting on school property," the principal barks at them. "I thought you kids would have learned this by now!"

Gabe and Andre keep their heads down. "We're sorry, Principal Craig," they both say in terrible unison.

"Well, sorry's not good enough."

"But they came and started it by hitting Andre!"

"You're both suspended for a week," Principal Craig announces. "Let's see if that will teach you enough of a lesson."

Gabe and Andre are dismissed, and walk from the school to wait for their parents. Gabe holds up a fist, and Andre stares at it and pushes it away.

"You just got me suspended," Andre says. Gabe pulls Andre's hand up to bump his fist and nudges his brother.

"Those bullies got you suspended." Gabe plunges his hands in his pockets. "What happened anyway?"

"No time to explain; there's Dad." Andre points to the familiar car pulling into the parking lot.

"Brace yourself," Gabe sighs. Their father pulls up to them, and they climb into the car.

"I hear you boys got yourselves suspended," their father says, driving out of the parking lot. "Another fight. You kids seriously need to get your acts together."

"I will when they stop bullying Andre," Gabe answers.

There is a tense silence in the car as they drive home. And then their dad speaks with a snort. "So, who won?"

"Us, duh," Andre remarks.

"That's my boys." Dad smiles. "Come on, I'll take you out for ice cream. If Mom asks, this never happened."

"Yes, sir!" Both brothers saluted.

"Not much of a punishment," God said from the stool beside Gabe. It didn't take him long to realize they were back in the bar again.

"That's just what my dad was like," Gabe shrugs. "Hard but fair. And encouraging one or two bad habits."

The silence builds between them.

Gabe can see a darkness in God's eyes, as he knows what to ask him next. It's as if God knows what that is

as well and might have been trying to distract him with
the memories, but Gabe isn't going to go without
asking it.

Chapter 7:

Best and Worst

Before getting to the inevitable, Gabe decides to lead into it slowly.

"Hey, God?" Gabe says.

"Yes, Gabe?"

"What's the best part about being God? The God of all beings, the Almighty One, and all that."

"The best part, huh?" God sighs. "I'm going to need a moment to think about that."

Gabe waits patiently. He pours another shot for each of them. He doesn't know what else to do with himself. Questioning God is the one thing he can think of to keep the conversation going. He's used to the fact that he can't leave the bar by now. Talking with God has been kind of therapeutic for him, fun even. Gabe has never been very religious despite growing up Catholic. He never thought in a million years that he would meet God in this way.

"Okay, I got it, the best part is gonna sound weird to you." God sits up.

"Lay it on me." Gabe faces him.

"When you guys leave this world and join me, you receive the gift of light," God explains with his hands once again. "Which pretty much means you understand the mysteries of the universe and can see the big picture for what it is."

"Wow, that's wild." Gabe's eyes are wide. "Like *everything,* everything?"

God nods with an almost giddy smile. "It's a clarity that you can't comprehend, and honestly, to watch people receive that, those who have genuinely tried to live the best life they can, is an amazing thing." God seems like he's holding back tears. "It gets me every time."

"I bet it does." Gabe smiles along with him. "It must be very satisfying to see those who truly deserve it get that kind of gift." Gabe's frowns when, once again, his thoughts go to why he came to this bar in the first place. He brings himself back to the conversation. "That sounds pretty good, actually, so why is everyone afraid to die?" He is acutely aware of God's expression. His face falls a little bit after hearing Gabe's question.

"Well, to be honest, it doesn't always work that way, unfortunately. As I'm sure you know, some people don't live good lives." God explains this with less enthusiasm than the other questions.

"Yeah, I've heard of a few." Gabe nods.

"Some live completely crappy, selfish, and extremely destructive lives that, under extreme circumstances, have caused heartache, pain, and even the death of others." God sighs. "When the light hits them, they understand all the mysteries of the universe, but they also understand all the pain they caused and the impact they had on others."

"They don't just go to hell?" Gabe furrows his brow. "Even the bad people meet you and see the light as well?"

"Of course they do. They may be misguided, but they still receive the same light that I provide for everyone," God says gravely. "All the pain and shame they feel causes them to isolate themselves from everyone else, and they live in this state where they are eternally alone and punishing themselves. It's not quite the fire and brimstone kind of 'hell' you guys think there is in the afterlife, but it's painful all the same."

"That doesn't sound as bad as fire and brimstone, but it still sounds terrible," Gabe says, rubbing the back of his neck. "So, does the devil exist? Satan and all that?"

"He's my brother, actually." God nods. "I made him in my loneliness during the birth of the universe."

"Wow, really?" Gabe has his mouth wide open in shock.

"Yes, I decided to create someone who could be my equal, but also my opposite. We get along very well, but he has his moments."

"What's he like?" Gabe catches himself. "Wow, I can't believe I'm sitting here, talking to God, and asking about Satan…is this a sin somehow?"

"You really need to lay off the television," God points at Gabe.

"Anyway, we're going off topic." God waves away the distraction as if it was really there. "Satan is someone you must meet to understand."

"If I had a nickel for when you're vague about something." Gabe leans his head on his hand against the bar.

"I am God. I can't tell you everything, can I?" God shrugs. "What I can tell you is that there is no hell other than the realization the bad people have about their lives and how bad they have been."

"Not going to lie, I was thinking you were going to say he's not real, just made up by the Biblical writers and Jesus."

"My son was many things, but he was not a liar." God waves a scolding finger at him.

"He did exist?"

"Yes, he did. The resurrection was his idea, by the way."

Gabe pauses and thinks to himself. "I wonder if those people knew the outcome going in, if they would change."

"I don't doubt some would." God shrugs. "But the way they live their lives is their choice, and it is not my place to judge while they're living."

"I don't know how I would feel learning all the mysteries of the universe." Gabe wonders to himself.

"Don't think too hard about it." God pats Gabe's shoulder. "It's way too much for a human brain to comprehend; you'll have your time, just like your father did."

Gabe sighs and he thinks about his father. He finds himself glancing at God and thinking about how much he reminds Gabe of his father. Mainly with personality similarities.

"You're thinking about him now, aren't you?"

"What? How do you know?" Gabe is flustered. "You can't hear my thoughts, can you?" Gabe gestures to his head.

"No, no, of course not. At least not down here. It wouldn't be fair." God holds his hands up defensively. "Don't worry. You just had that look on your face of deep thought, and I made an educated guess." God leaned a little closer like an old man leaning down to the level of a child. "Was I right?"

Gabe sighs and nods. "I was thinking about how you remind me of him, slightly," he said.

"I am indeed your father, I am the Father of all." God gestures his hands to everything in the bar. "Could be a 'dad' thing."

"I guess that makes sense." He looks up to God again with another question in mind.

"What were you thinking about? In regards to your father, of course." God poured himself a shot and drank it.

He turns to God.

"Yes, go on." God smiles. Gabe can almost tell that God knows he wants to ask another question.

"I want to know what is up with angels," Gabe says. "Do they actually exist? Do they take people to heaven? What do they do?"

"Well, they are my servants, and they are not dead people." God holds his hand up. "Let me just make that clear." Gabe nods and waits for God to continue. "They are only the archangels and others that I created to serve them."

"So, when we die, we won't become angels?"

"No, but I do admire the creativity behind that" God sips some more of his whiskey. "When you die, you just live with me and all the other souls who have passed on, watching the world from afar for the rest of eternity. Even the bad ones who must live with their terrible mistakes."

Gabe looks a little disappointed.

"Why the long face?" God asks.

"I was kind of hoping to be an angel someday." He pouts. God ruffles his hair.

"Sorry to disappoint you, kid." God laughs.

"Okay, final question for this topic."

"Shoot."

"What's the worst thing about being God?"

This question is something he had been expecting. Gabe could see that as God thought about the answer, his face betraying that fact. God thinks long and hard about this one.

"I'd have to say...the worst thing about being the father of all things, is watching you hurt each other. You guys try to make the best decisions for your situations and that's understandable. I don't regret giving you free will, but it doesn't make it any easier to watch. There have been whole years where I've wept watching what was going on down there. The entire duration of wars, especially conflicts that begin because of misunderstandings or simply one bad decision. The World Wars were one of the worst I had to watch you all go through. I get people joining heaven daily, but during those wars, I had millions."

"I can't imagine." Gabe gapes at him, propping his head upon his hand as he watches God speak again.

"And seeing the distrust, an epidemic that has always plagued you people, it was tenfold." God sits up straight and sighs. "I never expected you all to get along all the time, but attempting to wipe out so many simply because of their religion? Breaks my heart."

Gabe can see a tear or two escape God's eyes. He grabs a napkin and hands it to God.

"Thank you." He takes the napkin. "I sometimes forget humans cry, and I'm not used to it."

"You're possessing this guy?" Gabe gestures to the body beside him. "Is he a real person?"

God laughs. "No, of course not. I simply came down and made a human body for myself. I'm God, remember?" He waves his hand dismissively.

"Wow, I didn't think of that..." Gabe widens his eyes as if he hadn't at the moment. He actually hadn't realized it.

"You didn't because you never asked the question." God waves a finger at him like a scolding father.

"You do have a point there." Gabe points at him. Gabe bursts into laughter, and God does so at the same time. A big, booming laugh fills the room and echoes along the walls. Gabe feels the joyful energy he exudes, and it feels comforting. He relaxes and revels in the feeling. It's something he never knew he needed but appreciates just the same. In the way that a joke makes you laugh, or a warm hug calms you down. Those are the only things Gabriel can think of to describe this feeling. He heaves a sigh and he feels relief for the first time that day.

"And another thing, how am I not drunk and puking on the floor by now?" Gabe asks.

God laughs again. "You can hold your drink pretty well."

"I do have my limits, and I feel like I could have hit them by now."

"Fair enough. I suppose you ought to know, since you're wondering." God smiles. "I made this bar my own little pocket of time."

"So I could drink as much as I wanted…"

"But never be too drunk to be present in this conversation. I want this to be an experience where you can still feel calmed by the atmosphere and the alcohol, but it won't do you any harm," God explains, sitting back on his stool. He pours them both another shot and holds it up in another toast. "Here's to good conversation."

Gabe touches his glass to God's, and they both drink the shots down.

"I think we're in need of some more whiskey to shoot," God points out. Gabe looks at the now empty bottle and waves down the bartender.

"Hey there!" She comes up to them with a warm smile. This is not Marisha, Gabe observes, but someone he's never seen before. She was oddly familiar. "Have I seen you here before?"

"Maybe, I see you here a lot though," She winks. "Would you like another?"

"Oh, yes please," Gabe says politely. She smiles and picks up the empty bottle.

"I'll be back with that before you know it!"

Gabe watches her as she walks off, still trying to figure it out. "I guess she's new," Gabe shrugs.

"Or someone who only works once in a while," God suggests.

"That too." The bartender brings them back a new bottle of Jack and shoots them both a warm grin.

Chapter 8:

Why?

Gabe finds himself pondering on another few questions weighing on his mind. God takes notice of this and nudges him.

"You can ask; I know you have a few more questions," he says.

Gabe hesitates, suddenly feeling awkward about what he's asked before. What if God is getting annoyed at all these questions? Are these all dumb questions to him? Gabe sighs.

"Is everything okay? Circumstances considered…"

"Yeah, it's just, all of these questions I have for you feel so typical. I wish I had more profound things to ask…" Gabe trails off. God wraps his arm around his neck and pulls him closer, almost as if he was about to mess up his hair as a joking father would.

"When have you ever been a profound guy, Gabe?"

Gabe looks up at God as he speaks, and he lets him go.

God continues. "I know it's intimidating because I am God. I've been doing this for a while, but I want you to think about this like you're asking a distant relative about their life. This is a casual conversation; I don't expect anything less, kid."

Gabe considers this and glances up at God. "I don't know if that helps because you're God, or that was just what I needed to hear."

"All this God stuff is making me sound holier than thou. Even though I am, you can still consider me your friend here; go ahead treat me as such. Big questions and all." God nudges him again. "How does that sound?"

"I think I can do that." Gabe nudges God with his fist on God's shoulder.

"Come on kid, hit me with the next one." God waves him on.

"Okay, I got another one on that topic." Gabe holds a finger up.

"Lay it on me, bud." God holds his arms out wide.

"Why let kids get cancer?" Gabe asks. God crosses his arms and turns in the stool to lean his back against the bar as Gabe speaks. "I mean, why so young? They haven't even lived yet and you leave them vulnerable to die too early. It never felt fair to me."

"Is it ever too early to die?" God shrugs.

"I just don't understand it. I heard so many stories in the world where children can get cancer as babies and their parents go through hell watching their children sick with something that adults have more of a reason to get. Kids haven't even had the chance to either be good to their body or not to warrant that kind of illness."

"Cancer is never something that happens for a reason; there's never been anything specific that causes it, save for a few things you all have invented like tobacco and such." God leans his head to the side.

"Then why?"

"Because it's just another thing I created for you all to understand how important it is to enjoy your lives. Going way back to why I can't cure anyone, another reason is that if every disease could be cured by a wave of my hand, people who needed to wouldn't be living their lives to the fullest."

"So you allow children to get cancer and terrible diseases because you want them to know how short life is at a young age? Or for their parents to understand that?" Gabe stares at him, exasperated. "How fair is that? What about stillbirths and defects? Miscarriages? Why must children die?"

"Listen to me, Gabe." God sighs. "Life isn't all about just waiting for death to come for you. Sometimes, it will come for you when you least expect it, or even want it. You humans have many social norms that do not exist in the grand scheme of things. Children with defects are beautiful and valid as human beings, but humans have brought about standards of beauty and how each person should look in order to be respected. I create all those things because I believe they are meant to live or die just like all of you do. On the subject of stillbirths, they just aren't meant to come into this world. It's simple as that; it is the balance of things. The value of life is immeasurable when you never know when or how you're going to die. It's all a part of my grand plan."

"Well, what's the grand plan?" Gabe asks. "For all of humanity to suffer?"

"So much for not being profound." God pours himself a shot, then one for Gabe, and drinks his shot down. Gabe follows suit. "No, it's not that at all, as some of you guys could be led to believe."

Gabe knows very well that God knows what he's talking about, but Gabe clarifies as he knows God wants him to.

"I mean, you just mentioned some of it, so what is it? According to you, as the church says, everything happens for a reason because you planned for it." Gabe shrugs.

"Ah, I see, well, the plan is for you all to live and enjoy the life you have to the fullest you can." God faces the bar again and gestures with his hands. "Life is short for you guys."

"Okay, now *I* need you to be more specific with that." Gabe crosses his arms on the bar.

"Find your passion in this world, the purpose that resonates with your individual soul. Find a hobby that brings joy to your life." God shrugs. "That's all I planned for you guys."

"That's it? Just for us to find our goals and to live comfortably?" Gabe asks, raising an eyebrow. "You know that's harder than it looks, right?"

"Oh I know, that's why I worry about you all so much." God sighs. "Lots of people find comfort and purpose in worshipping me, and I do appreciate that, truly I do, but I understand it's not for everyone."

"Really? I thought everyone who doesn't worship you gets the 'hell' treatment, so to speak. At least that's what I remember hearing at church growing up."

"I can't change anything that people do, so a lot of stuff with those people that worship me has gone off the rails." God cocked his head to the side, staring at the bar. "But if that's what gets them through life, I'll still take them with open arms and they will realize everything once they get to learn the mysteries of the universe, as I mentioned before."

"So, even those who discriminate and treat people badly for not worshipping you?"

"All of you are my children, good or bad." God nods assuringly. "But I truly don't ask for much from you all."

"Is there anything else to it than that?"

"I want you to have relationships, make friends, find someone to love." God leans against the bar again, glancing at Gabe. "I gave you 7 billion other people on the planet to talk to, go find one you haven't met yet."

"Easier said than done; money is an issue."

"I saw when you guys invented the Internet; it was my favorite invention I witnessed. You now have the means to contact anyone in the world and meet someone you haven't met before."

"Yes, but that doesn't always work out," Gabe points out.

"A very good point." God waves a finger at him again. A proud smile spreads across his face, as if he'd hoped Gabe would have answered in this way. "You must expand your horizons to find the people you haven't met yet because they could change your life. And if it's bad, then you learn from it. Life is all about learning."

Gabe thinks about this point. God was really making him think here.

"Maybe there are things I haven't tried before that I could do," Gabe admits.

"Go for it, tell me." God waves him on.

"Maybe some traveling."

"I know there's more there; give me something more than that. Where would you want to travel, either alone or with your family; go for it."

Gabe takes a moment to think hard about what he would want to do. "Wow, I haven't thought about this before...I never really considered that this could be something I could do."

"Throw out all the thoughts and doubts stopping you, like money, opportunity, everything." God leans in and places a hand on his shoulder. "If you had any opportunity, forgetting the money issue, what would you want to do?"

It finally came to him.

"I would want to...take Anna to Europe," Gabe suggests.

"Where in Europe?"

"Paris, she's always wanted to go there," Gabe reminisces. "We talked about doing that someday when she was pregnant with Kayla. Back then we had a little more inspiration for our dreams."

"That happens when you have a child. Everything just feels exciting, despite the downsides." God nods.

"Exactly." Gabe nods along with him.

"What about with your family? Where would you want to take them?" God asks. "Again, no limits. Lay it on me."

"Hands down, Disney World. They always ask about wanting to go, but Anna and I simply never have the money. Even if we only went once in their lives, I know it would be worth it." Gabe sighs. "But for just traveling in general, I'd like to take them to The Cayman Islands, or somewhere tropical. Maybe even Hawaii."

"That place is very beautiful, and it's thriving so well. Why there?"

"My kids are very into nature, at least Jeffery is. The others pick at him for it sometimes, but I'd love for them to meet and learn about marine life through some sort of scuba diving tour. Just so they can see at least some of the beauty you made for them and that Jeffery can already see himself," Gabe explains. "Something for them to see the animals in real-time, in their own habitat, rather than a zoo."

"That's very beautiful. I bet they would love that, all of your children and your wife."

Gabe realizes something as he tells him these things. "This is making me realize how much I've let my family down, how much I could have provided for them that I haven't and probably never will…" Gabe fiddles with the shot glass in his hands and then pours another shot. He knows he won't feel the way he expects he should from the alcohol, but it's the one thing he can think of. He feels the weight of God's hand on his shoulder again.

"Hey, it's okay, son," God says with a small smile. "Let's get away from your family for a moment and focus on you. What would you want to do? Where would you want to go?"

Gabe takes the shot and drinks it back, staring at the ceiling.

"Push all those negative thoughts from your mind for a moment and think about what you love." God speaks to him slowly.

"You know you sound like one of those meditation apps right now, right?" Gabe snickers without humor.

"It works." God shakes his head. "Now, go for it, think."

"I would want to…" And then it hits him. "I would want to find a Delorean DMC-12 from that *Back To The Future* movie and just drive it as far as I can, seeing everything."

"That's a very interesting choice."

"It was always my favorite car; growing up, it was the thing that made me want to be a mechanic." Gabe smiles to himself. "Ever since I saw that time machine blow through the road, leaving flames in its wake, I knew I wanted that car. Of course, they're rare now and hard to find."

"That's wonderful, Gabe. That sounds like the perfect road trip. Do I detect some soul searching involved?"

"Maybe there could be, but I'd just like to drive one." Gabe shrugs. "I know it's not the most life-changing thing, I'm not going to save the planet while doing this, but it's… what my dad and I always talked about."

"He liked cars as well, didn't he?"

"Yeah, he took me to see the movie at a drive-in theatre when I was a kid and I was hooked." Gabe sighs again. "I guess I would want to feel closer to my dad again. That's not crazy, right?"

"Of course not; it's exactly what I would want for you, and any one of my children." God spreads his arms wide. "The secret to life is to live it. It's a winding path and everyone is different. All with their own walks of life and ways that they could make themselves happy if they had the means, but of course, there is also comfort in finding your own ways to live your life to the fullest."

Gabe feels an immense feeling of comfort from what they just spoke about. Meeting God isn't as scary as he would have thought.

Chapter 9:

So, What's Next?

After all that has gone on tonight, Gabe looks at God and asks, "So, where do we go from here? What's next?"

God gets up from the bar. "Well, Gabriel, you tell me. You've been the one asking questions all night, playing games, drinking, etcetera." He sits down at a table and gestures to the chair across from him as he speaks. "What's going on with you? What are you avoiding?"

"Me? Avoiding something?" Gabe pours himself one more shot and downs it before bringing the bottle to join God at the table.

"Mhmm." God nods. "Now we've had our fun, learned about me and why I do what I do; it's your turn."

Gabe sighs. "I guess this is the point of you finding me, isn't it?"

"It's why I'm here, yes." God nods again. "There's no rush. Take your time. Why don't we start with why you're here in this bar."

"Don't you know that? You are God."

"Yes, I do know all, but not what you're thinking." God takes his index finger and brushes the tip of his nose.

"Well, I just like coming here. It's close to home, and I know people here." Gabe shrugs.

"So, this place is like a second home to you? How so?"

"It's just so inviting and relaxing. Might also be because it's partly a family restaurant as well as a late-night bar. It's been around ever since my dad took me here as a kid in the 90s."

"What makes it so inviting?"

"The atmosphere, the wait staff are all so sweet, the people are great; Doug does a great job with this place."

"Ah, Doug the bartender?" God smiles. "What's he like?"

Gabe is grateful the questioning didn't begin with something emotional. God's been having him flip-flopping all night. It was a relief to think God was trying to soften the blow.

"Doug's a great guy. Always there and willing to listen." Gabe snickers. "And to make sure you don't drink too much. He's the ringleader that looks out for everyone, including his staff. I saw once that he chewed out a drunk, tough customer that was mouthing off to one of his waitresses. I remember the guy left; the whole place clapped."

"Sounds like an upstanding guy." God nods.

"He is."

"I'm starting to understand what you like about this place." God leans closer. "I'm glad to know it's not just the alcohol."

"Of course not; the alcohol is the pleasure, but the added bonus is the social atmosphere." Gabe gestures around the room. "What would this tavern be without the conversation? The drinking games, the sound of the balls on the pool table, the clink of glasses as they're put away, the loud laughing from across the room."

"I'm glad this place can be a place of solace for you, all things considered."

"It is. I think it helps that it's not just a bar, but a family restaurant too. It's equal parts one thing and another."

There is a silence between them again as they take in the sights and sounds all around them. "I think I see what you mean now." God nods with his lips pursed in agreement.

"Right?"

God looks over at him, unable to figure out how he should say what he will in the next moment. Gabe can almost sense the depressing topic coming based on God's expression.

"Do you still have that nightmare?"

"What? I don't know what you're talking about." Gabe furrows his brow in confusion, trying to mask his reaction from God, but it was futile.

"That nightmare where you relive the moment you found out your father died." God leans back, watching him. Gabe continues to try and hide his reaction. "You can try to hide it, but you know what I'm talking about."

"It comes around now and again...trauma does that." Gabe grits his teeth.

"Yes, it does, but this is something you can get past as you talk about it and face it more."

There is a silence between them for a few moments. Gabe can feel the tension rising in his chest, the anticipation for what God could be asking him next, that this must be the talk he was hoping to have all along, but he allowed Gabe to avoid it.

"I think I want to share one more shot first." Gabe glances at God.

"If that will help, then of course I will." God smiles. Gabe tries to pour the shots, but the bottle only has a few drops left.

"Wow, looks like we finally did a number on this one," Gabe chuckles.

God gestures and both glasses fill with whiskey. Gabe cocks his head.

"I'll admit, I forgot you could do that, and here I was pouring the shots." Gabe shakes his head and holds his glass up to clink it against God's.

"I figured it was more natural-feeling and more relatable to use the bottle, so I just let it happen," God admits. God drinks his shot down, and Gabe hesitates, and then follows suit.

"That was me avoiding it again, wasn't it?" Gabe looks down at the glass.

"As I said, no rush." God waits patiently.

Gabe takes a deep breath and heaves a long sigh. "I have been drinking too much, but it helps to dull the pain. Of the nightmare, the reality of my father's death, and everything I have that's unresolved around that..." He can't look God in the eye. "I know I need to work to provide for my family, but I'm miserable at my job."

The emotions are starting to take over as Gabe continues slowly. God still listens and waits quietly. He sits back, his hands folded in his hap, watching Gabe as he speaks.

"I feel like I'm drowning every day, and I don't know what to do." Gabe starts to feel tears building in his eyes, but he blinks them back. "Sometimes, I feel like they would be better off without me."

"I can assure you, they wouldn't be," God reassures him. "Why are you miserable at your job?"

"Because it reminds me of my dad, and what could have been, and how I failed."

"You're not a failure, Gabe." God leans forward slowly and places his hand on Gabe's forearm. "When did this all start?"

Gabe takes a moment to gather himself before he continues. The presence of God's hand on his arm is comforting, but he feels he doesn't deserve the hopeful look in God's eyes. He clears his throat and continues.

"It started sometime after my dad passed away. I bet you know how he died without me saying it." Gabe glances at God.

"Yes, but I want you to say it." God nods in encouragement.

"He had a sudden heart attack six years ago." Gabe has to fight harder to hold back the tears. He clears his throat again.

"Were you with him when it happened?" God asks.

Gabe shakes his head. "I was walking in from work and Anna came to the door and told me Andre, my brother, had called." Gabe swallows, and his voice breaks. "I remember he showed up at the house that night and we didn't say a word when I opened the door; he just hugged me."

"I'm sorry you had to find out that way, Gabriel." God nods slightly.

"That night, we went off to the bar and felt better afterward," Gabe recalls.

Gabe found himself transported back to that night six years ago. God's presence at his side reminds him of what this is, another memory. Gabe is standing in the same bar he and God have been sitting in for the whole night thus far. He walks around, seeing the same patrons as usual, but less of them and six years younger. Finally, he sees himself and Andre sitting at the bar together, toasting to their dad with whiskey shots and drinking them down.

"Some things never change," God remarks.

"I hope you're not referring to—"

"Oh, no, kid, no. I was just talking about whiskey."

An awkward silence hangs in the air as the white noise of the bar continues around them.

"Okay, point taken." God walks towards the two brothers sitting at the bar.

"Okay, okay." Andre sways a little as he points somewhere around Gabe. "Funniest moment with him."

"With Dad?" Gabe thinks for a moment.

"I got one," says Andre.

"You remember that one time He dressed up as Fred Astair for halloween?"

"He dragged Mom around to dance with him until she finally agreed to."

"We laughed like crazy and we peed our pants!*"*

Gabe snickers and laughs. "Nah, I got one better. That one time he came home from work and told us not to tell Mom anything."

An understanding was made between them as they both remembered the same moment.

"Oh my God, that fuckin' giraffe!" Andre laughs loudly.

"He came home with an inflatable giraffe from the party store and he blew it up in the backyard like a Macy's Day Parade balloon!" Gabe wheezes.

"Mom was so pissed she gave him money to stay at a hotel for the night so she wouldn't have to deal with him." Andre chuckles, trying to hold in his laughter. They sit there laughing for a few minutes and then take another shot each.

In the next moment, they are both sobbing.

"I can't believe he's gone," Gabe sniffles. "He was fine yesterday. How is this not a bad dream?"

"It's not, but I wish it was."

"Hey, you guys okay?" Doug appears in front of them, changing out the bottle of whiskey for a new full one. "You look pretty down."

"Hi, Doug." Gabe waves through sniffles and sobs. "Our dad passed away."

Doug's eyes are wide. "No, really? I really loved that guy…" Doug leans in and takes a shot himself. "You guys discussing good memories with him?"

They nod, still wiping tears from their eyes.

"Didn't you two know each other?"

"He used to come in here from time to time." Doug smiles to himself. "In fact, I believe he was the one to introduce you two to this place, wasn't he?"

"Yeah, he did!" Gabe sits up. "He took us here when Andre got his big job."

Gabe pats Andre on the back, a little harder than his sane mind would have normally allowed. Andre coughs a little.

"I remember that," Andre nods, clearing his throat. "What's your favorite memory of him?"

"Whenever he came and talked about you two." Doug nods.

"He came and talked about us?"

"Not all the time, but the few times he did. He made my day. This job isn't as easy as it looks, but I digress," Doug says. "This is my favorite one."

"Tell us!" Gabe chimes in.

"Okay, keep your shorts on!" Doug waves for them to calm down. "He came in one time after one of you had your first kid, I think it was Gabe. He had come in for Andre's first, and when

he came in for Gabe's daughter, he was giddy like a kid at Christmas."

"That's Dad." Gabe took another shot.

"He talked about how scared you were and how proud he was of you. He was drinking, just like you guys were, and raving about your daughter and how much she looks like your wife. It was like stepping into a view of your life I've never seen, Gabe. It was always a nice escape from the mundane life of this job." Doug holds his hands up. "Not that I don't love seeing you guys, anytime."

"Lemme pay the tab and tip you, man. That was beautiful." Gabe pulls out his wallet.

"No, stop, this is on the house. You guys need it tonight." Doug pushes Gabe's hand away. "Now, you kids behave yourselves."

Doug waved a finger at them and they held up shots.

"Yes, sir!"

Gabe laughs to himself as he watches.

"We got so drunk that night Doug had to kick us out because we were falling over ourselves by the end. Somehow, we knew everything was going to be alright. I remember that vividly, despite the state we were in."

"It's good you two had that time together," God says with a small smile.

"My dad was the reason I went to school to become a mechanic, to work on cars, and learn about something I loved that I could do for a living. He was my main encouragement. We used to work on cars a lot when I was growing up." Gabe's eyes fill with tears when he can't hold them any longer. "Losing him was the hardest thing I ever had to do, and I never even got to tell him I loved him one last time."

"I'll have you know, he does love you very much, and he knows you love him," God assures him.

"I bet he thinks I'm a failure," Gabe sobs.

"You're not, Gabriel; you did try."

"After he died, I did try to keep going, just because I knew he would want me to, that he would want me to do the work that he had inspired me to do. I even considered starting my own mechanic business, but I let it fall through," Gabe continues.

"How did that happen?"

"I don't know why I'm telling you this; you know it all." Gabe looks up at him.

"You explaining this is all for you. I'm your moral support," God explains. "It's better for you to let it out in words and emotions. I gave you them for a reason."

Gabe nods and keeps going.

"It fell through because...I gave up." Gabe shrugs. "I thought it would be the one thing I could do to thank my dad for all he did for me, but his loss hit me so hard that I couldn't get out of this rut where I felt like it wasn't worth it when he's not around anymore. Almost like I relied a lot on his encouragement, and now that it was gone, there went my mojo."

"And where did you go from there?"

"I started drinking a lot, and I couldn't stop." Gabe holds his head in his hands. "Andre had gone through having a problem with drinking right after Dad died, but I stayed stronger. I made sure I could be his strength through our loss, and to support our mother. He got through it with AA meetings, but knowing how bad it was for him apparently wasn't enough to stop me from doing it to myself."

"Sometimes you lose control, and that's okay." God pats his arm. "What else happened? Were you drinking heavily for six years?"

"No, heck no." Gabe shakes his head. "It started slowly. I began having a drink after work, and then, as time went on over the years, and especially after my mechanic business venture fell through a couple of years ago, after my grandparents passed away within months of each other, I spiraled."

"And why is that?" God asks. "What was it that made you feel like you needed it?"

"I just needed something, anything to help me cope with everything that was going on. I began to feel better drunk than I did sober because I couldn't feel anything. I couldn't feel the grief I felt daily for my dad and my grandparents. The pain of what could have been with

my dad. All that pain was too much for me...and still is,
I suppose."

"Did you drink in front of your children? Were you
drunk around them?"

"I did drink in front of them at dinner, but I only did
my heavy drinking here at this bar, or late at night." He
sniffles, thinking about a certain event. "I tried not to
be drunk around them, I really did, but..."

"What happened?" God has a knowing look on his
face, his eyes still soft.

"There was a time where I was at Kayla's dance recital
drunk and I passed out in the bathroom. Anna had told
me to go because she couldn't, and I let Kayla down
that day." Gabe rubs his eyes and takes a sharp intake
of breath. "She didn't speak to me for a week until I
apologized to her. And even when I did, I could see it.
In her eyes, I knew she didn't believe me. That's when I
decided I would never get drunk at home again. I
wouldn't let them see me like that."

"And what about your other children? And Anna?"
God inquires.

"My other kids are too young to understand what I'm
doing, thank God..." Gabe catches himself. "Sorry,
name in vain."

"No problem, you can thank me, I'm right here." God
winks. "Go on."

"Yeah, well, Anna knows. She had an alcoholic father that left her." Gabe grabs a napkin from the table, wipes his eyes, and blows his nose. "I don't know why she hasn't left me yet, even though she should."

"I would assume it's for the children." God nods slowly. "They still love you, don't they?"

"Yeah, somehow, even Anna. She's always seen something in me I never could." Gabe smiles a little.

"How did you two meet?"

"We were high school sweethearts that blossomed into long-term lovers after college," Gabe says. "We kind of took a break when we left high school because we couldn't have a long-distance relationship since we went to different schools, but we kept in contact. Once we both graduated, she wanted to try again, and about a year later, I asked her to marry me."

"I remember seeing that wedding; it was beautiful." God smiles.

"Yeah, it was." Gabe finds himself looking back to that moment. The loving look in her eyes as she cried, gazing into his like he was all she ever wanted. "She was always someone I thought about, even when we weren't dating. We called once in a while; we hung out with friends together. Once we got back together, I realized I couldn't live without her. I still couldn't. God, what have I done to her...she doesn't deserve this."

"She does deserve you, if you are willing to be worthy of her." God pats Gabe's arm again, and then folds his arms on the table.

"I've been a terrible husband and father, brother...and son..." Gabe breaks down in his hands. He forgets about all the people around him and just lets it all out. "I haven't dared tell my mother about this, but I bet she knows."

"She knows, and she worries about you," God says. "Andre made sure she was told."

"She must be so disappointed in me. How can I go on, God?" Gabe begs for an answer. Anything for him to figure out how to get out of this mess. God moves his chair on the side of the table closer to Gabe and pulls him into his arms. Gabe leans his head on God's chest. God holds him similar to how his dad would when he was sad as a boy.

"It's going to be okay, son. I'm proud of you," God says quietly.

"What is there to be proud of..." Gabe whispers.

"I am simply proud of you for being alive and for being my son." God rubbed his back assuringly, and Gabe sobbed into his chest. After he calms down a little bit, he pulls away from God and wipes his tears.

Gabe thinks about how great this opportunity is, how much he's learning about God and the universe.

"I never thought I would ever get to do this, to actually meet God," Gabe laments. God glances over at him.

"I thought you never believed in me." God nudges him.

"I mean, I might have. When I was a kid going to church, I knew there had to be someone somewhere watching us." Gabe stares up at the ceiling. "But as I grew older, I just lost interest. Something I knew could still be real, but couldn't be at the same time."

"How does it feel to know it's all real?" God inquires, gazing at Gabe to gauge his reaction.

"If I'm honest, I'm a little relieved, but also a little angry."

"Why angry?"

"Because I wish I knew before. This could have helped me a lot over the past few years."

"I'm sorry, kid. I should have come sooner, but you know what?"

"What?"

"I always had faith you could turn it around someday, with or without my help." God wraps his arm around Gabe's shoulder. "I saw that you needed guidance, so here I am."

"So, what should I do now?"

"Ever heard of AA? Alcoholics Anonymous? One of my favorite of your people's inventions." God smiles. His face falls when he sees Gabe still frowning. "What's wrong?"

"I have heard of it…I know what it is, my brother uses it," Gabe admits. "And I haven't considered it."

Gabe sees God is taken aback, but he stays neutral in his tone. "Why not?"

Gabe shrugs. "I don't know, I—" Gabe sighs.

"Take your time; as always, no pressure to speak," God says. Gabe nods and takes a minute. He takes a deep breath.

"I guess…I'm scared."

God nods a few times, glancing at the bar. "What are you afraid of?"

"I don't know. I just don't think it's going to work for me."

"You think you're too far gone?"

"I could be; I don't know. I have considered it, don't get me wrong…" Gabe stops to take another minute to collect his feelings. He takes a deep breath again and sighs. "I'm just worried I'm going to try it and just give up right away. And then go back to how I have been for so long."

"Do you like drinking?" God asks.

"Yes, I do, but I can't forget how it's been ruining my life…"

"What did it do for Andre?"

"It helped him; not easily, but it helped him." Gabe shrugs. "But he's always been the most adaptable one. I saw a few failures in my life and I just began drowning myself."

"Well, I think it's ultimately your choice, and I hope you know I will still love you, no matter what you choose." God wraps his arm around him again. "No matter what."

Chapter 10:

Last Call

Gabe sighs. Taking in the conversation he and God have just had in the past...however long it's been.

"How are you feeling?" God asks.

"Much better, but I'm still a little nervous." Gabe sighs.

"Nervous about what?"

"Everything; seeing Anna after going out to drink. Again. Dealing with Andre, facing my mother..."

"It's going to be alright." God nods. "You'll see."

"Last call!" the bartender calls from the bar.

"Oh, how time flies," God remarks. "That's my cue to skedaddle." God gets up off his stool and waves with a nod to Gabe.

"Wait, not yet!" Gabe begs, holding God's sleeve. "Please, can't we have more time? Can you do that with your God powers? You made this pocket for us to talk..."

"I'm sorry, son, it's time for me to be going." God shakes his head and gently takes Gabe's hand from his sleeve. "Oh, and one thing, I almost forgot. You won't remember any of this once you wake up."

"Wake up? Have I been asleep this whole time?"

"No, but I will be putting you to sleep so you can wake up back before you meet me." God gets up from his chair.

Gabe balls his hands into fists and stands up from his chair with such force that the chair slides back and then falls with a loud bang. "I finally get to talk to you after living an entire life even truly wondering if you exist, and now you won't even let me remember?"

"It's better this way; trust me, kid."

Gabe runs fingers through his hair and glares at God. How could he lie to him like this?

"What was the point? This whole night? If I'm not going to remember anything we talked about, why even bother?" Gabe shouts, walking up to him as he rants.

God stands unblinking and unphased by the whole interaction. Gabe becomes even more anxious the more God doesn't speak.

"Please, answer me." Gabe's eyes fill with angry tears. "I need you; I can't do this alone."

God steps closer to him and places his hand on his shoulder. I think you might have one more question for me, the one you've been wanting to ask me this whole time but you've been too scared to ask it."

Gabe looked inside himself, everything he'd been feeling before this and during this experience. He looks up into the eyes of God and asks him. "Am I going to be okay?"

"Yes, Gabriel, I promise you." God pats his head.

"How?" Gabe whimpers. "How will I be okay forgetting the time we've had, the reality I finally understand?"

"I know for a fact you'll be okay because I've seen this before." God smiles.

"What?"

"This isn't the first time we've talked, bud." God pats Gabe's shoulder and folds his hands in front of him.

"I'm still confused…" Gabe furrows his brow, trying to figure out what God is talking about. "If it was just like tonight, I wouldn't remember it, would I?"

God sighs and smiles. "Do you remember six years ago when your dad died and you and your brother hit the bars?"

"Yes, that night after we heard the news, we went out drinking…" Gabe cocks his head to the side.

"And then the next morning you woke up and felt comforted?"

"Yes…"

"That night, you, Andre, and I stayed up all night just like tonight until you guys broke down and felt reassured that you were gonna be okay." God nods once. "This night is no different, Gabriel. Which is why I'm sure you'll be okay as well this time."

God gestures to the place they were just sitting at the bar. Gabe finds himself watching him and his brother at the bar six years ago in the memory God showed him. This time he saw God there in the same clothes, sitting between them and holding them both close as they cried.

"One more shot? For the old man?" Andre offers.

"Yes, I'm down, How about you God?" Gabe agrees and both of them look at God. God is already pouring the shot.

"Way ahead of you kids," God hands them the shots. "To great fathers everywhere!"

The three of them cheer and drink down their shots.

"Now, tell me about him, what's your favorite memory?"

The memory fades and Gabe is standing before God again, looking up at him.

"And back then you did the same thing…" Gabe realizes. "That's why we don't remember it."

"Exactly, so once I leave, you will feel the same way, if not better."

Gabe understood now; that's why he felt that way. He always felt this immense feeling of comfort when looking back on that night. As if that night had been a warm hug.

"I always thought it was the alcohol that helped me that night," Gabe muses.

"For that, I regret." God sighs. "I realized I should have thought you would have confused that feeling for something I didn't intend. This bar was a comforting place for you two, so when you came back, I knew I had to make up for that mistake."

"So, why can't I remember that? Why won't I remember this?" Gabe looks up at him, hoping to hear a different answer than he expects.

"The answer to that is simple, bud; free will," God explains. "I need you guys to be able to choose your own paths. To not rely on me to help you through your problems. Only I decide whether it is a good time to come and help you, but it will only be remembered in impressions, and not memories. Everything you've learned here will change you, but not in any way you will be able to explain or understand."

"So, I will remember how I felt by the end of tonight?" Gabe asks.

"Precisely."

"I see." Gabe lowers his head, disappointed at the point God is making and how much sense it makes.

"You knowing for sure that I exist compromises that. You can't have faith without a little doubt; that's one trick I've learned over the millennia," God continues. "But know this, I have always been there for you, Gabriel. All those times when you found inner peace, that calmness or inner strength you needed but were struggling to find, that was when I was with you the most."

"You were?" Gabe looks up.

"Yes." God nods, placing his hands on both of Gabe's shoulders. "I was there with you, cheering you on when you were working hard to keep your father proud after he passed away. I stood beside you when you planned out your mechanic business. I even sat with you after your grandparents died."

"Somehow, I think I always knew someone was there," Gabe confirms. "I always assumed it was my father, or even my grandparents, but it was you all along."

"Yes, Gabriel." God smiles, walking closer to hold Gabe's face in his hands appraisingly, like a father would admire his son. Gabe's tears fell from his eyes.

"Will you always be with me?" he sobs.

"I am and always will be with you, through all the dark and the light that you see yourself in. You will never be alone." God nods warmly. "In case I'm busy, though, I promise one of us will always be there."

"Us?" Gabe is confused and he narrows his eyes.

Gabe suddenly notices that the bar has gone eerily silent. He sees everyone in the bar has stopped talking and is looking at him and God standing in the middle of the bar.

"We'll be here for you...Booger Butt," a voice behind the bar says, causing Gabe to turn and God's hands to drop from his face. He takes a closer look at her and realizes she looks strikingly familiar.

"G-Grandma?" Gabe stutters, taking a few steps towards the bar.

"Yes, Gabe, it's me," the bartender says. "I bet you don't recognize me like this. I used to look like this when I was younger."

"Well, I'd say you've always been this beautiful." Gabe looks and sees a man walk up to the bar and climb over it to stand beside her. They share a brief kiss that makes Gabe want to cringe, but he can't look away.

"Is that you, Grandpa?"

"Hello, Booger Butt." Young Grandpa smiles and wraps his arm around Grandma's shoulders.

"Gabe, say hello to all your ancestors." God gestures around the room to all the people sitting in the bar.

Gabe looks around and sees so many people that he has seen in old pictures. He even sees his great grandparents, who he'd never met. He sees people from way back in his lineage, even back to medieval times, where one is in a suit of armor. They all wave at him as he turns. He takes it in and waves at them all.

"Wow, I can't believe how far back we go…" Gabe gasps. He feels a tap on his shoulder.

"It's good to see you again, son."

Gabe freezes. He knows that voice well, but he can't believe he's hearing it. He turns in the direction it came from and he sees his dad standing there.

"Dad?" Gabe's voice sounds small to his ears. "Is it really you?"

"Yes, son." Gabe's dad glances at God with a nod, and God nods back. "It's me."

Gabe jumps into his arms, surprised but grateful to be able to feel his father hug him back.

"I've missed you so much," Gabe sobs, pulling away and looking at his dad. "I think about you every day."

"How's Mom doing? How's everyone?" his father asks, crying as well.

"Mom is great; she's doing amazing, always keeping you alive in her stories to your grandkids. They all miss you as well, even the young ones," Gabe explains, waving his arms as he does so.

"That's wonderful. I miss her too, and all of them." Gabe's father sighs. "Anna as well. I always thought she was a wonderful girl; you're so perfect together."

"Thanks, Dad," Gabe snickers.

"I'm sorry to have left you in the way I did, son." Gabe's dad places a hand on his shoulder. "I would have wanted more time in the end."

"I only wish I could have been there to say goodbye, or to have the time to," Gabe says. Gabe's dad glances at God and then back to Gabe. "To tell you I love you one last time."

Gabe wipes the tears from his eyes with his sleeve, then God passes him a napkin again.

"I always knew you loved me, even without you saying it."

"I'll take the time now. I love you, Dad."

"I love you too, son. Do you think I could have a few moments with him?"

God doesn't hesitate when he nods and gestures for Gabe to go on.

"Take all the time you need." God smiles.

Gabe walks with his dad to a table and they sit down.

"I'm sorry I became this way; it must have been hard for you to watch us go through your passing like this." Gabe sighs.

"I left you all without warning and outside of my control, and yours. It's understandable, though it does make me sad. I almost felt responsible," Dad says.

"You're a hard man to get over."

"What has Mom been up to? You still asking her about our story?"

"All the time; you two have always been an inspiration." Gabe winks.

"I'm glad," Dad laughs.

"Did you dance with her at Tina and Harry's wedding so you could be with her?"

"I never told her, but yes." Dad smiles. "I went for the wedding and left with my heart in her hands. I did feel a little bad that her boyfriend broke up with her over me, but she assured me it was mutual."

"If it's any consolation, I appreciate the coupling."

"That's a weird one, but I'll take it!"

"Are you happy, Dad?" Gabe asks. "Where you are?"

"I am, wholeheartedly. I always wanted to tell you how proud I am of you." Gabe's dad cups his cheek. "For the man you have become. Sure, you're having a setback, but I know you can bounce back just like I watched you do before. Can you do that for me?"

"Sure, Dad, I will."

"And go ahead and start that mechanic garage of your own. You have the skills; I made sure of that!" Dad waves a finger at him.

"I will, as soon as I'm clean." Gabe nods and hugs his father.

"Remember, we're always with you," Gabe's dad says, and nods to God. "And we always will be. I'll be watching you shine, son."

Gabe hugs his dad one more time.

He turns to God. "I know I won't remember this, but I want to thank you, for...well, everything."

"I want to thank you, as well, for the pleasure of your company. This has been fun. You asked a lot of the questions everyone else does, but not a lot of them ask about my opinions and feelings as well, so I commend you for that, son." God smiles. "I'm glad you got to see your father again. I'm sorry you won't remember this."

"It's all right; this is enough." Gabe glances back at his father and holds his finger up. "One more thing."

"Anything."

"Can you give me any heads up for what's going to happen since I won't remember anyway?"

"Keep coming back; it works if you work it." God nods and waves.

"Wait what?"

Then, everything goes black.

Gabe opens his eyes and he's blinded by the sunlight. He looks around and finds himself in his and Anna's bed, but he's alone. He's confused, and wonders how he got there.

"What happened?"

Epilogue

Gabe distinctly remembers being at the bar, but he's glad to be home. A warm feeling exudes from his brain as if something had come to him while he was sleeping and injected something into his body to make him feel comforted. He needs to find Anna. He jumps from the bed and stumbles. His head is pounding. He leans against the dresser and one of his kids arrives at the doorway. It's Jeffery and Meaghan staring at him, and they start to giggle.

"Daddy is in his underwear!" they say in jumbled unison.

"Underwear Daddy is coming to get you!" Gabe rushes to the door, and the boy and girl run away screaming and giggling. Gabe sighs and puts some clothes on. He needs to find Anna.

He goes down to the kitchen and sees Anna at the kitchen counter making some sandwiches for the kids. No one else is in there, so he walks in and snakes his arms around her waist from behind. He successfully catches her off guard and he feels her jump.

"Holy shit, you scared me, Gabe." Anna looks back at Gabe as he kisses her shoulder and leans his chin on it. "You're up early...and sober."

"I have something to talk to you about," he says, holding her close.

"Okay, well, you wait right there while I pack up this last sandwich." She holds up one half of a bologna sandwich, and Gabe nods.

"I can wait." Gabe turns his head to lean on her back. "I'll just take a nap here." He then proceeds to pretend to snore, as if she's taking too long.

"Ugh, stop." She groans and finishes her task. He lets her go so she can turn around. "What is it?"

Gabe catches her lips on his as she turns to him. He kisses her once, and then twice, pulling away on the third one.

"Stop, you still taste kind of like alcohol." She covers his mouth when he pulls away. "What's with you today?"

Gabe places his hands on either shoulder and runs his hands down until he's holding both of hers. He strokes his thumbs along the tops of her hands and sighs, looking her in the eyes.

"I know I haven't been acting like the best partner and husband these past few years," Gabe says. Anna is quiet; he feels her watching him as he glances down at her hands. "When we got married, I vowed to take care of you and be there for you, and I haven't been. I've been ditching you and the kids to sit at a bar drinking myself under the table and showing up to work the next day drunk."

"And you've been fired from that job, haven't you?" Anna asks, shaking her head. "Gabe…"

"What I'm trying to say is, I know I have a problem." He looks her in the eye, tears beginning to form in his. "I want to work on it. I really do."

"Oh, Gabe…" Anna groans. "Can I just?"

"Sure." Gabe closes his eyes and waits for the slap he knows is coming. It impacts his face with a soft *thwap*. He opens his eyes and rubs his face a little. "Ah, jeez…yep, I deserved that…"

"You know how hard it's been for me, watching you go through this alone?" Anna remarks, her own tears falling now. "Seeing you find your answers in a drink rather than your wife?"

He feels Anna's hands leaving his and then a tissue on his eye. He holds her hand there and opens his eyes.

"I know, I can't imagine." He bows his head. Her other hand brings his eyes to hers. He smiles slightly. "I am so sorry for what I've done to you. You never deserved any of it."

"Promise me you will actually get help and stick with it," she demands, her voice cracking.

"I swear on my father's grave," Gabe confirms. Anna nods, understanding the meaning that has for him. "Okay." She pulls him into her arms for a tight hug. "For the record, I always knew you were drunk going to work, leaving to go to the bar every night." Anna says slowly. "It felt like I was losing you and I just had to watch it happen. Every time I tried to tell you to stop, you wouldn't listen. But I'm glad it looks like someone at that bar finally got through to you."

"Ew, ugh." Kayla's voice comes from the doorway, then Jeffery and Meaghan emerge as well.

"I think they saw us." Gabe nods.

"I think they did," Anna agrees. "What shall we do?"

"Cooties." Gabe makes a gesture like his hands are crab claws and runs after the kids, grabbing Jeffery and Kayla into a big hug while picking at their clothes with his hands. Anna does the same with their youngest while they all giggle and laugh together. Anna and Gabe share a knowing look before letting the kids go and telling them to get ready for school.

Anna and Gabe help their kids get ready for school and send them off to the bus. As Anna is about to leave and go to work, he stops her.

"Hey, sweetie, can I ask you something?" Gabe slips his hands into the pockets of his pajama pants.

"Sure, what is it?" she asks.

"Do you know when I got home last night?" Gabe scratches the back of his head. "I can't remember how I ended up in bed."

"I mean, if you were drunk, how could you remember?" She shrugs. "All I know is you weren't there when I went to sleep, but when I got up, you were there. I just assumed you dragged yourself home as you have before."

Gabe nods. "You're probably right…"

"Why do you ask?" She's rummaging through her purse, making sure she has everything she needs.

"No reason, I was just curious."

"Okay, well, you have a good day. I'll be home this evening," She walks up to him and plants a kiss on his lips.

"Okay, you too. I'll see you later." He waves. "Love you!"

"Love you too!" she answers, and then walks out the door, closing it and locking it behind her.

He is then left alone in the house, with his own head. He messes with his hair and pulls his phone out of his pocket and sits down at the kitchen table with a cup of coffee.

He is scrolling through his phone to find Andre's number. He taps the phone icon and the call goes through. It feels like an eternity before Andre answers.

"What do you want?" Andre snaps immediately. "Haven't you done enough?"

"Hey, simmer down, man. I just wanna talk," Gabe answers.

"Wow, you actually don't sound hungover for once in your life." Andre sounds genuinely surprised, and it prompts Gabe to smile.

"I wanted to know if you wanna meet for lunch? I have something I want to talk to you about," Gabe offers. "Now that I do have some spare time these days…"

Gabe isn't expecting Andre to agree, but he's hoping he will. The silence on the call is deafening before his brother finally answers.

"Yeah, why not? Come meet me at the office and I'll take you to that deli you like," Andre suggests.

"Nah, let's go to that burger place we used to go to with Dad," Gabe counters. "Ben's, I think?"

"Good, I feel like I could use a good burger." Andre clears his throat. "I'll come to pick you up around noon."

"Sounds good."

"See you then, bye."

"Bye."

Gabe hangs up the phone and sighs. That was easier than he expected, but he knows this is something he needs to do.

Gabe waits on the porch of his house, sitting on the stairs. He stares down at the ground, remembering the last conversation they had, how he was in a much different headspace than he is now. Something in that bar changed him last night, and he didn't know what it was, but he was grateful for it.

Gabe sees Andre emerge from through the door and walks down the driveway to meet him.

"Hey," Gabe greets him, climbing into the car.

"Hey," Andre answers. He doesn't look at him as Gabe closes the door and puts on his seatbelt.

The silence lingers between them for the entire drive; the only sound is the ambiance of the radio playing music in the background. Gabe doesn't need the conversation, at least not yet. He knows the silence is warranted, and Andre is not going to want to talk to him yet, but Gabe is trying so hard to keep quiet. Instead, he watches the buildings and people as they drive by. They arrive at Ben's Burgers, and Andre parks the car. Andre offers to buy, so Gabe finds them a booth, watching Andre at the counter. It doesn't take too long for Andre to arrive with their food and they set it out for themselves.

Gabe holds his burger up to Andre in a toast.

"Come on, just like old times," Gabe says. Andre glares at him and sighs, touching their burgers. They both dig in and groan in unison at how great the burgers taste. Gabe chuckles, and Andre laughs along with him, the tension loosening between them.

"God, I've missed this place," Andre admits. Gabe nods.

"Best burgers in town," Gabe says with his mouth full. He takes a sip of soda and sighs. Once they are both finished with their burgers, they sit, nibbling on the fries.

"So, what prompts this?" Andre asks.

"What, I can't spend a lunch date with my brother?" Gabe shakes his head like the sentiment was obvious. It is not obvious to Andre.

"You know I'm not talking about that." Andre was serious.

"I wanted to apologize to you...about last night, about everything." Gabe leans forward and dips a couple of fries in ketchup then eats them.

"Wow, did the drink finally knock some sense into you?"

"Let's just say, I did a lot of thinking last night, and I think it's time I made up for the mistakes I've made. I apologized to Anna this morning, and here I am hoping you will accept it as well." Gabe looks his brother in the eye. "I'm sorry I was drinking so much and couldn't keep a job. I took advantage of you, and I should have been taking the help you gave, but I didn't. I hope you can forgive me."

"I will only accept your apology if you get help."

"I will—"

"And stick to it." Andre held a scolding finger between them. "Can you promise me that?"

"I promise." Gabe nods. "I want to fix myself and do better for you and mom and my family."

Andre seems to see the genuine nature of Gabe's words and sits back, nodding.

"That bar changed you last night, didn't it?" Andre states. Gabe shrugs.

"I guess something must have happened. I woke up in my bed this morning with this big reassured feeling that I will be okay." Gabe glances at his brother. "Do you remember that time we went to drink at that tavern after Dad died?"

"Yeah, we drank each other under the table," Andre chuckles. "There was a lot of laughing and tears that night. I remember Doug had to kick us out."

"Do you remember the feeling you had the next morning?"

"Yeah, I do. It was as if Dad was right there giving me a big hug." Andre clears his throat.

"That's exactly how I felt this morning." Gabe shakes his head. "I can't describe it any other way."

"How's Mom doing?" Gabe asks. "I feel like I haven't seen her in years."

"It's been months," Andre corrects him. "She's still doing okay. Thriving with her retirement community. Who would've thought she would ever enjoy being there?"

"Dad left her that reservation so she wouldn't be alone." Gabe nods. "I think she took a lot of comfort in that."

"You should come with me to visit her this weekend," Andre suggests.

"Yeah, why not? I'd like that a lot," Gabe nods. He watches as Andre eats a few more fries, and he musters up the courage to ask the question. "So, when you had your problem...what helped you through it?"

"Ever heard of Alcoholics Anonymous?" Andre leaned forward.

"Only in those cheesy ads on TV."

"Ellie gave me an ultimatum when I was in your shoes six years ago, and I've been going ever since." Andre stares at the fries and nods to himself. "The best decision I ever made. Saved my marriage and my life."

"I think I'd like to try that out." Gabe eats a few more fries himself.

"Good." Andre smiles. "I'll take you with me to the next meeting they have tomorrow."

"Wait, what? Tomorrow?" Gabe gapes at him with wide eyes. "That's a little soon."

"The sooner the better." Andre finishes up his food and gathers up their garbage before Gabe has even finished his fries.

Gabe is thinking about his mother. About how she would be feeling about all this. He decides to go and see her before Andre picks him up for the meeting. He drives up the driveway to her house and parks the car. He's never been so nervous to see his mother in his whole life. He finally builds up the confidence to get out of the car, lock it, and knock on the front door of the house. Small barks make themselves known, alerting the owner of the house that there is a visitor. He can hear his mother's voice as she shushes the dog. He can feel the footfalls as she walks towards the door. She unlocks it and opens the door to see him on the other side. She's holding a small, tan-furred pomeranian, Sir Biggles, in one arm, and holding the door with the other.

"Oh, Gabriel, what a wonderful surprise!" Her smile fades. "Did you break the law or something?"

"No, no way, Ma. I just wanted to come and visit you." Gabe shrugs, his hands in his pockets.

"I know you got fired again." She still keeps the hardness in her voice, but it softens with sympathy.

"I did."

She looks him in the eye for a moment and then waves him inside. "I've missed you so much!" She pulls him into a tight hug. "I thought I'd lost you."

"I'm okay now, Mom." Gabe hugs her back.

He follows her inside and closes the door behind him. She carries the dog to the kitchen and calls back to Gabe. "Do you want anything to drink?"

"Some water would be nice, thanks, Ma," Gabe calls back, wandering to the living room. It's filled with pictures of her and Andre and all her grandchildren. Gabe sees a picture he'd seen many times before of his parents. His mother and father are standing in 1980s attire, early '80s, Gabe recalls them saying. She was shorter than he was, but not by a lot. You wouldn't be able to tell because, in the picture, his father is leaning forward with his tongue out in a funny face. His mother, subsequently, has her thumbs in her mouth and is pulling them outward to make her own version of a silly face. It's here where Gabe realizes how much Andre really does look like his mother. They have the same eyes, same nose, even the same face structure. Gabe, on the other hand, being the older brother, looks more like their father. Gabe always denied this fact, citing that his father was more handsome, his mom in agreement.

"Go on, sit down." His mom gestures for him to sit down on the couch. She puts a coaster down and places his glass of water on it. She sips the cup of tea she brought for herself, and Sir Biggles jumps up onto the couch beside her, staring at her. "So, what brings you here to grace me with your drunken presence?"

"You'll be happy to know I'm not drunk today."

"Good, I hope you've learned your lesson." She sips her tea again, giving him a side-eye.

"I have, believe me. I wanted to come here to apologize. For everything."

"That's a tall order. Making me worry, treating your wife like dirt and your kids the same. It's a disaster." Mom shakes her head and takes another small sip of her tea.

"I know. I went to the bar last night, and this morning, I woke up feeling like a different person." He nods, smiling at his mother. "I've even asked Andre to take me to an AA meeting tonight."

His mother raised an eyebrow and cocked her head to the side. "You changed your mind overnight?"

"I don't know how, Mom, but I did." Gabe shrugs. His mother studies him and nods.

"You go to those meetings and stick with them, you hear?" She says, pointing to him.

"Yes, ma'am." Gabe nods.

"Good, they helped Andre a lot after your father died." She shakes her head.

"How have you been, Mom?" Gabe asks.

"It's still been an adjustment since your father died. Living alone isn't the best, but it has its moments. Little Biggles keeps me company." She pats the dog's head.

"It was all so sudden, wasn't it? One day, he was fine, and then suddenly, that massive heart attack." She chokes up at the memory.

"I know, it shocked us all," Gabe admits. "Did you ever tell me how you two met?"

"Well, you know he asked me to dance at Aunt Tina's wedding, and I was sold. He was so handsome back then." She grabs an old picture from the shelf, the exact picture Gabe was looking at. She giggles to herself. "He made me laugh so hard I could cry while also making me so angry I could divorce him. We were literally inseparable after we met."

"Could you tell me the story?"

Mom waves her hand and shakes her head. "You've heard it a million times, you should be sick of it by now," she says.

"I'm not." Gabe shakes his head. "I wanna hear it again."

Mom searches his expression and nods. "Okay. Well, we were both invited to my sister's wedding, Tina, your Aunt Tina and Uncle Harry's wedding. Back in '85 or something, I think. He was a friend of Uncle Harry's. Anyway, I was there dancing on the dancefloor with my boyfriend at the time. He came around and danced with us, your father, I mean. My boyfriend introduced him to me and said that he was Harry's friend. I was charmed, of course. I noticed him at the ceremony and congratulating the happy couple. We all danced together for a few songs until my boyfriend had to go sit down, as drunk as he was at the time. I got him some water and stayed with him while your father and I talked. He was so charming and funny and very handsome; I almost forgot I had a date with me!"

Mom laughs to herself, and Gabe joins her. He revels in the way his mother lights up while telling the story. That is the exact reason he loved hearing it. He knew Andre could see it too, despite his complaints about the story being told too many times.

"Dad always was a charmer, wasn't he?" Gabe remarks.

"Yes, he was." His mother is beaming as she goes on. "Not long after, about a few months, that boyfriend and I broke up. We had it coming, so no harm no foul; we continued to be good friends even when he got married, but anyway, I finally agreed to go on a date with your father."

"Where did you go?"

"To the movies. Went to see some popcorn flick that was famous at the time, but we spent more time in our own little world. We got kicked out of the theatre, of course." Mom takes a sip of her tea.

Gabe shakes his head and glances at his hands before looking back up at her. "What did you do?"

"We couldn't keep our hands off each other. And we shouted at the movie, about every stupid detail that bothered us that we could think of. Don't get me wrong, we loved what we saw of the movie, we just...had a bit to drink."

Gabe laughs again. "You two were brutal."

"We went on a few more dates before I took him to meet your grandparents. I remember he was dressed up like he was going to prom." Mom snickers. "He was so stiff; not even water could soften him until the end of the night."

"What did Granny and Grandpa think?"

"They loved him. Granny took some warming up to, of course, but he passed her tests, whatever they were." His mother rolled her eyes. "You know how Granny was."

Gabe chuckles to himself. "Yes, I do. She was a spitfire. No one could get by her easily."

"Didn't it take her a while to approve Anna?"

"Well, let's just say it was a process." Gabe winks at his mother. "What happened next?"

"Well, we rented an apartment together, and then bought a house, and he asked me to marry him." Her smile is warm as she remembers. "And the rest is history."

"How did he propose?"

"Oh, he was the most romantic when he wasn't trying. But on that night, he really did try. I came home from my shift at the hospital and he had lit up the house with some candles. I distinctly remember the candles were all different, some random ones I had around the house and hidden away for Christmas and things like that." Mom waves her hand, dismissing her sidetracking. "Anyway, the candles lead to the kitchen, where he had made dinner for us. Chicken parmesan." Mom nods confidently.

"He never cooked for us…"

Mom shakes her head. "Never had the time; that's why I did it more often. He wasn't too bad of a cook, I must say." She raises an eyebrow.

Silence falls between them and Gabe can see tears welling up in his mother's eyes.

"After he died, I didn't know what to do with myself. He was my whole world, Gabe, as I know he was yours." She leans forward and grazes her fingers on his cheek affectionately. "You take after him so much. I remember seeing you two working on cars in the garage for hours."

"You would bring us snacks and juice," Gabe remembers. "There was no way we would leave that garage, other than for pee breaks, until we were satisfied."

"Both you and your father were stubborn as hell." His mother shook her head. "And I wouldn't have had it any other way."

Gabe sighs. "It's not fair what Andre and I did to you, making you worry about us...our drinking problems. You never deserved that, and I want you to know that I'm going to fix myself. I'm going to be attending every

AA meeting with Andre until I can go back and continue to face Anna."

"It was terrible; you two should be ashamed of yourselves…" Mom snaps, then softens. "I'll only accept that apology if you stick with it. You remember how long it took for Andre to keep going to those."

"I had to go pick him up and drive him to keep him accountable." Gabe shakes his head, his leg twitching up and down until he consciously stops it. "Until I started doing this to myself."

"Is he coming to pick you up?"

"Oh, shit, I forgot to tell him I was coming here." Gabe pulls out his phone and texts Andre. After his brother replies, Gabe announces to his mother. "He's going to pick me up later."

"Would you like some lunch? I bet you haven't had anything to eat yet."

"*Mom,*" Gabe groans. "I did eat breakfast."

"If you say so. Come on, I'll make you some grilled cheese." Mom gets up and motions for him to follow her. Sir Biggles barks once and follows them, his tail a wagging floof as he walks. "I know it's almost three in the afternoon, but I wanna make you something."

There's a knock at the door while Gabe and his mother are enjoying a late lunch. Gabe offers to get the door. He opens it and sees Andre on the other side. Somehow, Gabe didn't expect this.

"Oh shit, is it that time already?" Gabe looked at his phone. Andre shakes his head and enters the house.

"Nah, I just wanted to come early and hang out with Mom for a little while before we go," Andre says. Gabe nods.

"She's in the kitchen."

"Well, look at this surprise." Mom does the least convincing secret wink. As if she had no idea Andre was coming."

Gabe rolls his eyes at his mother's attempt at a joke. She totally planned this. For Andre to show up an hour early.

"I know now we definitely got our humor from Dad…" Andre snickers, gets himself a glass of water, and joins her and Gabe at the table. Mom glances between them, a somber look in her eyes.

"Ma?" Gabe leans toward her to see if something is off.

"Oh, it's nothing; just ignore me and go about your business." Mom waves her hand again.

"You can't just sit there and look at us like that without us questioning it." Andre glanced from her to Gabe and back.

"It's like you two are going out to have fun together…" she says, a reminiscing tone to her voice. "I just think it's been so long since I've seen you two getting along like this."

Gabe glances at his brother, and Andre does the same.

"Yeah, I guess it has been a few years," Andre scratches the back of his neck.

"It's just an AA meeting, Mom…" Gabe shrugs.

"Your brother is trying to help you get on the right track, just like he got himself back." Mom tears up. "It's just so sweet."

After sharing a few laughs with Mom to make her feel better, Andre and Gabe were on their way.

"You let me know how it goes, okay?"

"Sounds like I'm going back to school for the first time." Gabe smiles and hugs her.

"Oh, let her be." Andre hugs her too and goes to start the car.

"I'll come by again tomorrow morning," Gabe assures her. "I'm out of a job for now, so I'm thinking I'll have some time on my hands while the kids are at school and Anna is at work."

***

Andre and Gabe drive up to the place where the meeting is being held, a local church in the area. Gabe finds the building familiar.

"Wait, isn't this..?" he asks as they walk from Andre's car.

"Yep, the church Mom used to take us to when we were kids." Andre nods, locking his car and pocketing the keys in his jacket pocket. Gabe walks with his hands in the pockets of his jacket.

"What a way to come back here, as an alcoholic," Gabe mutters.

"As an alcoholic seeking help," Andre corrects him. "There is something to say about that."

"I'll let you know, once we're done here," Gabe remarks. Andre laughs, and holds the door open for him. And then, this overwhelming sense of fear takes over and Gabe stops in his tracks. Andre notices this and holds the door for another person and pulls Gabe aside.

"Hey, what's up?" Andre's expression is twisted in concern. "Are you feeling okay?

"I just...What if this doesn't work?" Gabe stares at nothing as he speaks. "I don't know if I can do this..."

Andre places a hand on his shoulder. "I know what you're feeling; I've been there," he states. "You're going to your first AA meeting, and you're terrified. Of being vulnerable, of acknowledging you have a problem in front of strangers. And that's okay. We all go through it. But I need you to remember that you're not only here for yourself, but for Mom, Anna, your kids."

Gabe considers Andre's words. "Okay, let's go in before I change my mind."

Andre opens the door and Gabe walks into the church.

The walk through the church to the basement is a trip down memory lane to a time where Gabe learned great morals, but didn't care for the experience of being in a big building where an old man spoke for an hour and put him to sleep. Walking through here also makes him think of his dad. They held his funeral here, and Gabe's parents got married here. Even Andre himself got married here. This building holds a lot of good and bad memories, but he feels different being here now.

He again feels what he had when he woke up the morning before after being at the bar, the feeling of comfort, as if someone is giving him a warm hug and is telling him everything is going to be okay. Today, he believes it more than ever.

Upon entering the basement, Gabe remembers playing here as a child while his parents spoke with other parishioners upstairs. It is a little dated, having not been touched much for about 20 years, but it's still homely. Chairs are set up in a circle, and a table sits at the far end of the room with cookies, cheese, crackers, coffee, and tea. There is a small gaggle of people mingling around, drinking coffee and eating the food.

Gabe takes a deep breath, and Andre claps his hand on Gabe's back, almost knocking the wind out of him.

"Everyone, this is my brother, Gabe, and he's going to be joining us tonight!" Andre announces. Gabe stands frozen, his hand comes up in an awkward wave.

"Hello, Gabe!" everyone says, waving, and then going back to their conversations. One woman in particular comes and greets them.

"Gabe, this is Michelle; she runs these meetings." Andre gestures to her.

"It's wonderful to meet you, Gabe." Michelle shakes Gabe's hand, and Gabe nods.

"Good to meet you too," he says, side-eying his brother. Michelle nods and gathers everyone together to take their seats. Gabe nudges his brother in the arm.

"You know I'm gonna kick your ass later, right?" Gabe whispers.

"No swearing in the house of the Lord." Andre winks, pulling Gabe with him to find chairs for them.

The meeting starts with Michelle introducing.

"Welcome, everyone, my name is Michelle, and I would like you all to join me in a brief moment of silence and a prayer." She bows her head, and some join her and others don't. After the moment of silence, she begins reciting the Prayer of Serenity. Gabe sits there, still a little uncomfortable. He knows the prayer, but he and a few other people just listen as it's spoken. It was something he had seen on some prayer cards at church growing up, but never really paid attention to. As he listens he thinks about the words and what they mean for this group and himself. When the prayer ends, it breaks him out of his reverie and he brings his mind back to the meeting.

"Okay, now, before we start, who is here for their first meeting?" Michelle asks the room.

Gabe sees some other people raise their hands, and Andre nudges him. He raises his hand as well, and Michelle nods.

"I want you all to remember there is no pressure to participate in this meeting. We are all humans and all sharing the experiences we have of being alcoholics. We don't shame or discriminate here. This is a safe place," Michelle explains. "If you just want to sit and listen, that's fine as well. If any of the newcomers want to introduce themselves, you can take the time now. Again, no pressure at all."

Gabe hesitantly raises his hand again after another glance at Andre, who nods him on.

"Yes, you." Michelle smiles.

"H-Hello, um, my name is Gabriel, but you can call me Gabe," he says slowly. "This is my first meeting, and uh, I'd like to just sit here and listen for now, if that's okay."

"Hello, Gabe, and welcome," Michelle says. "Let's all welcome Gabe."

The room erupts into a semi-enthusiastic drawl. "Hi, Gabe."

He's thankful that the rest of the newcomers similarly introduce themselves. As they do so, Gabe feels a little of the pressure lift from his shoulders. He sits silently as other members take their turns speaking. Gabe listens carefully as they tell their stories.

"I'm Harry, and I'm an alcoholic," one man with a white beard says. The room greets him, and Michelle asks him to tell them anything he's comfortable with. "My wife left me a couple of years ago. She said if I didn't get the help, she would end the marriage, and at the time, I didn't, so she took the kids and moved in with her mother. Now that I've finally kicked my butt out to get help, I told her I was coming here. She agreed to talk."

Gabe found himself paying extra attention to this story. Harry continued a little longer, talking about what made him drink, and Gabe felt especially related to his situation. He was slowly building up courage as the other stories were told and ended.

"Hi, I'm Jane, and I'm an alcoholic. But I've been successfully sober for two years." The room greets her as she speaks and claps at her confession. "I lost my husband to alcoholism, and I knew I didn't want to do that to my kids. These meetings really have helped me a lot." Jane nods, and Gabe joins in clapping with everyone else.

Michelle asks one last time if anyone would like to share, and Gabe takes his chance. "I'll speak." He raises his hand.

Andre gapes at him and pats his shoulder.

"Please, go ahead, Gabe." Michelle smiles.

"Hey, I'm Gabe, Andre's brother, and I'm...I'm an alcoholic." Gabe is greeted by them all, and he tells his story. About his father, about Anna, and how he's surprised she hasn't left him even though he deserves nothing less...everything that he's had bottled up and drowned in a drink. Once he's finished, his eyes are flowing with tears, and Andre has his arms around him, giving him a tight hug.

Michelle holds another moment of silence and recites "Our Father" to end off the meeting.

"That concludes our meeting for today; let's say the motto everyone." She stands up and gestures for everyone to speak with her.

"Keep coming back, it works if you work it," the room all says together, Andre as well, at Gabe's side. It touches Gabe in a way nothing had before as he looks around the room and sees everyone beginning to socialize.

It felt more real than ever, and he believes every word of the phrase. He would continue coming back as if his life depended on it.